MISTAKEN IDENTITY

Miss Fishbank had come forward now and placed a hand upon Susan's shoulder. "There, there, my dear," she said soothingly. "I'm sure there is nothing to fear." She peered at Lord Merlin closely. "Why," she said in tones of wonder, "It's Nicholas Chance, isn't it? Of course, you're Merlin now. My, how you've grown! There, you see, my dear? I've known Lord Merlin since he was a boy! There's nothing to fear from him, I assure you!" Her tone was soothing, and after a moment, Susan was able to look up at him, if only just.

"I'm so embarrassed," she said at last. "Just so embarrassed. But I can't marry you! I can't!"

"Please, do not start crying again, it is excessively tiresome," Audrey said. "No one is going to make you go home, or marry Lord Merlin, although I am a little vexed with you for allowing me to think that it was *old* Lord Merlin you meant, not this one!"

A LADY
OF
FASHION

REBECCA BALDWIN

HarperPaperbacks
A Division of HarperCollinsPublishers

This is a work of fiction. The characters, incidents, and
dialogues are products of the author's imagination and are not
to be construed as real. Any resemblance to actual events or
persons, living or dead, is entirely coincidental.

HarperPaperbacks   *A Division of* HarperCollins*Publishers*
              10 East 53rd Street, New York, N.Y. 10022

Copyright © 1994 by Helen Chappell
All rights reserved. No part of this book may be used or
reproduced in any manner whatsoever without written
permission of the publisher, except in the case of brief
quotations embodied in critical articles and reviews. For
information address HarperCollins*Publishers*,
10 East 53rd Street, New York, N.Y. 10022.

Cover illustration by Bob Berran

First printing: June 1994

Printed in the United States of America

HarperPaperbacks, HarperMonogram, and colophon are
trademarks of HarperCollins*Publishers*

❖ 10 9 8 7 6 5 4 3 2 1

Precisely at the fashionable hour of five o'clock, a high perch phaeton, drawn by a pair of matched grays, swept through the gate of Hyde Park and proceeded at a smart pace down the Row. The elegant lady at the reins, attired in a driving coat of claret bombazine with a smart toque rakishly tilted over her dark curls, turned to the handsome young military gentleman at her side and smiled, seemingly oblivious to the two dowagers in the barouche moving at a much more sedate pace down the gravel pathway.

"Isn't that Lady Wellford?" one of the dowagers asked the other, her lips curving sharply downward in deep disapproval. "Driving that phaeton! In the park, no less! That woman is entirely too dashing by half! If she doesn't watch herself, people will start to say she's *fast!*"

Her companion, who had been leaning forward to

squint at the couple in the offending vehicle, gasped, gripping her companion's sleeve for emphasis. "Isn't that young Major Shelby she's got up there with her? And him a good ten years younger than her! She'd better have a care!" She sniffed with disapproval. "Lady Wellford had better watch herself. She's getting a reputation!"

"They do say—" the first lady began eagerly, then bent to whisper the rest of the story in her friend's ear.

Evidently, whatever she said was very scandalous, for her friend gasped, all her chins wattling at once as she placed a gloved hand against her lips. "No!" she finally managed to exclaim, trying to hide her pleasure in this tidbit. "Too shocking for words!"

"I had it from the very best source," the other lady said.

"And what happened after that?" the first woman asked eagerly.

"He left cards on all London and went to South America. They say his heart was completely broken."

Her friend clucked her tongue. "Outrageous, shocking!" she said, fanning herself fiercely. "That Baron Wellford's widow should act in such a way!"

"They say he left her so well off she can do just as she pleases!"

"Fancy that! Why, I heard—"

"Audrey, those old tabbies in the barouche are staring at you," Major Shelby informed his companion as they came around the drive again.

Lady Wellford laughed. "And very likely saying some very nasty things about me in the bargain! Not only is my high perch phaeton too daringly fast, and my clothes too dashing, but now I have been seen driving with the handsomest hero in London by two of the town's biggest gossips! I am afraid that the sight of you must have been too much for them. I do you no credit, Giles!" No longer in the rosebud blush of youth, she was still young and beautiful, with a neat figure a little above the medium height and an expressive pair of dark eyes that always seemed to survey the world just a trifle haughtily. Their effect was offset by the decidedly upturned curve of her lips. Lady Wellford was generally acknowledged to be a beauty and a wit.

"On the contrary, Audrey, you do me a great deal of credit," exclaimed her companion. "I am being seen with the beautiful, the dashing, the exciting Lady Wellford! I am doubtless the envy of every buck on Rotten Row to be up beside you!" These words were spoken with such passionate sincerity that Lady Wellford had to cast a sidelong look at him, to be sure he was not teasing her.

But Major Shelby never teased. The youngest hero of the recent Spanish campaign (he had been mentioned in the dispatches) was almost painfully earnest as he turned to look at her profile. He could not help but feel intoxicated by her presence. Giles was quite sure that one morning he would wake to find that the woman who sat beside him had been a dream, such was the depth of his youthful infatuation. "Audrey, I had hoped that we might be able to have a serious discussion today. I am sure you are aware of my feelings—" he began.

"And I am sure that you are aware of mine, Giles," Audrey said quickly. "You know that I have a most sincere *tendre* for you, Giles, but—"

"I know! I know! It's only been a fortnight since we met, and you are a little older than I, and you never intend to marry again. You have said all of these things. But—"

"Isn't that Sylvia Godolphin over there on the footpath?" Audrey asked quickly. "Do wave at her, Giles, and smile!" She suited her words to her actions. "There is someone you need to be civil to—she can do you a great deal of good in the War Office."

"Hang Sylvia Godolphin!" the Major sighed. "It's you and I that we need to talk about, Audrey! I thought when we came out for this drive that for once, I might get you alone. It seems to me that you are forever in company, and that I never have a chance to talk seriously with you—alone!"

"Perhaps that is because I despise being alone and enjoy having people around me," Audrey replied lightly, looking straight ahead. As much as she enjoyed *looking* at Major Shelby, with his handsome face, adorned by a dashing cavalry mustache, his golden hair, his broad shoulders and well-formed legs, so perfect for military attire, there were times when she did not enjoy talking to him. He could be so *serious!*

He sighed, looking at her from blue eyes that could have melted a heart harder than Audrey's. Nonetheless, she reminded herself sternly, her heart had been tempered by high fires. If only he were not quite so handsome, nor such a hero of Spain! Why, it was almost her patriotic duty—

She quickly reached out and touched his hand. "I am sorry, Giles! It's just that I am not used to—" Before she could finish her sentence, her attention was caught by a dark-haired man on horseback riding past in the opposite direction. For just a second, their eyes locked, and she was conscious of his enigmatic smile and his rugged countenance. He touched his hand to the brim of his hat and disappeared from her line of vision before she could react.

"That's odd," she said. "Giles, who was that? That man who just saluted us? No, don't turn around, that would be rude."

"That fellow on the big black gelding? Never saw him before in my life," Giles said impatiently. "Audrey, if only you would at least listen to me—"

"He looked so familiar, and yet I cannot place him. There are so many people in town for the victory celebrations—well, it doesn't matter." Audrey shrugged. "One meets so many people."

"I can't say that I like strange men staring at you," Giles said mulishly.

"Oh, it's not me he was looking at, I am sure! It was probably the phaeton. Men are always so shocked, you know, to see a mere female handle a team. And I must say, I am proud of my grays," Audrey was quick to reassure him.

They drove along in silence for a few minutes before she spoke again. "Giles, I wish I could make you understand. I just do not want to marry again."

"Is it that your heart is in the grave with your late husband?"

A bubble of laughter escaped from Audrey's lips. Seeing that Giles was profoundly shocked, she swiftly exclaimed, "Oh, no! Not, you understand, that I was not sincerely fond of Wellford, for I was! He was a *very* kind man, and I was extremely fortunate. It is just that he would have been extraordinarily surprised to hear anyone ask if my heart was in the grave, for no one was less full of romantical notions!"

"Still, Audrey, to be married to a man nearly thirty years older cannot have been easy for a young girl!"

"I was seventeen, and it was an arranged match. Try to understand, Giles, that I was thoroughly unhappy at Bleakfriars Abbey. My brother and sister-in-law were—well, it doesn't bear thinking about! But, you see, Aldus was kind, and good, and as rich as a golden ball, and liked nothing so much as indulging me with everything I saw and took a fancy to have. I have been very spoiled, you see. "

"It's money, isn't it? I know that I can never hope to offer you all the material advantages, but—"

"It is *not* money! Aldus left me extremely well off, you know. And he trusted that I would have enough common sense not to be taken in by some fortune hunter. No, Giles, my dear, your money or lack of it is not the problem at all!" Audrey said forthrightly. "Besides, I have the greatest faith in your ability to rise in the military to great glory and full honors. It's just that I do not choose to marry again! Oh, dear, we were so happy before this all came up . . ."

Instantly apologetic, Giles turned to her and tried to seize one of her hands in his own. "Forgive me! I—"

"Please do not grab my hands when I'm driving! " Audrey said sharply. "You will overturn us!" With some effort, she righted her horses. "I am sorry, but you of all people should know better, Giles."

Major Shelby's handsome brow darkened. Suppressing a sigh, Audrey applied herself to charming him out of his sulks and back into his usual sanguine temper. She succeeded, in the end, only by promising him that she would have dinner with him that evening.

"And now, my dear, I must set you down," she said, "For I see my dear friend Madam Hart on the path and I know she will go into a Cheltenham tragedy right here and now if I do not take her up this instant!"

"That a lady like you could claim an *actress* as your best friend never fails to—" Major Shelby started to say, then thought better of it. Experience had taught him that Lady Wellford did not take kindly to criticisms of her friendships or her doings.

The famous tragedienne (currently appearing with great success at Drury Lane in *The Tragical History of Mary of Scotland*) was indeed taking the air in the park. In spite of the clement weather, she was draped in scarves and shawls, which she believed gave her an antique air, enhancing her classical features. They also served to disguise her slight *embonpoint,* the result of her great love of sweets. She was accompanied by Sir Peyton Rudge. A corpulently ruddy gentleman in a bright brocade waistcoat who closely resembled his dear friend, the Prince Regent, Sir Peyton enjoyed a friendship of long standing with Madam Hart.

Audrey brought her team to a halt beside the pair. Sir Peyton bowed deeply, his stays creaking just a little. He swept Audrey with a roguish look. Sir Peyton had been quite the rake in his prime, some twenty years ago. "Ah, it is Lady Wellford, who puts the stars to blush," he called. "And of course, the young hero of Spain," he added generously, with a nod at the major. "Taking the air in the park, what? Amazing, the people you see these days. We just bowed to General Blücher himself!"

"Audrey! Imagine running into you here! I really must try getting up early more often. I had no idea that people actually went about in broad daylight," Madam Hart saluted her friend. The famous voice that had thrilled theatergoers for the past decade rang out through the park. She smiled at Giles, with an eye that missed nothing. "And how are you, Major? You look extremely handsome today," she purred.

The major, who considered Sir Peyton an ancient fop, and Madam Hart a bad influence, muttered something that was civil, bowing to the actress and nodding curtly at the Regent's great friend.

"I saw you waving at me and I knew you would want me to take you up," Audrey said to Madam Hart, who, to her credit, looked blank for only a moment before making a reply.

"What? Oh! Oh, yes, I do so want a turn around the park. Fresh air, so *bracing*. I am sure it must be so good for one, but it casts me in mind of the country, and I despise the country. Peyton, Audrey will set me down by the gate directly. Do be a dear and wait for me there!"

"Ah," breathed Sir Peyton, ever affable. "Yes, quite so. Exercise, you know," he informed them all solemnly. "My doctor says exercise is quite the thing and that I should walk a turn or two every day. Thing of it is, plays havoc with the shine on my boots, don't you know, this outdoors walking." All eyes turned down to look at his dazzling footwear, decorated with large silver tassels. Clothes, Sir Peyton believed, made the man. "Well, dear boy, climb down, and you and I shall walk about a bit, on the strut! Have a look at all the pretty Continental ladies in their summer finery, what? By Jove, isn't that the Duchess of Dino I see over there?"

With reluctance, Giles climbed down and assisted Madam Hart into his seat. "Till tonight," he said.

"Tonight, my dear. I count the minutes," Audrey replied with one of her dazzling smiles. She pressed the tips of her fingers lightly against his cheek then picked up the ribbons, driving away at a smart pace.

"Good Lord," Emma Hart said frankly. "I can never look at that boy without feeling faint. Such beauty should be outlawed! It's simply not safe to allow anyone that young and that handsome to be walking on the streets. And he seems quite mad about you, my dear! Doubtless all the debutantes are casting jealous eyes at you."

"Yes, Giles is quite handsome," Audrey replied. In spite of herself, she chortled, just a little. "It is wicked, isn't it? He's only twenty-four, and I need not scruple to tell you that I'm almost thirty!"

"Almost?" Madam Hart's eyebrow went up slightly.

"I won't tell if you won't, Emma! Not that you can't give me five years, my dear. I only wish he would accept this *affaire* for what it is and stop pressing me so close!"

"Audrey, I know you as well as I know myself, and I know all the signs. You needn't scruple to tell me that you don't feel a *tendre* for him, because I won't believe it. You may try to tell the world that you are hard-hearted and cynical, but *I* know you better than that. Now is it love or is it good old-fashioned lust? You can tell me!"

"Well, I do feel a decided partiality for him. I mean, I *look* at him and—"

"I know. One wants to gaze and gaze." Emma sighed and ran a fringe through her fingers. "And all those war heroics, mentioned in the dispatches—it's overwhelming."

"If only he would not press so hard. He is asking me to marry him!" Audrey exclaimed. "That is why I asked you to come up and take his place beside me. I had to put an end to the subject, and he would not take a hint!"

"Well, what's wrong with that? He's not the first suitor you've had since poor Wellford died, and you could do far worse than a young man who's head over heels in love with you," Madam Hart advised. "As far as I can tell he's not a fortune hunter or a quiz or the least bit *nacky*. So what if he is a few years younger than you? You know, Audrey, you really should marry again. Wellford's been dead for nearly eight years."

"Why should I marry again? To have some man control my life and my fortune? For you know, the way the laws are set up, if I were to marry again, my husband would have complete control of my life and my money. Now, Emma, there are certain advantages to being a widow, you must admit. I have a considerable degree of independence, for one thing, For another, I like my life. I have my dear old governess Appie to bear me company and keep me respectable, I have my house on Half Moon Street and my house in the country, my little *pied-à-terre* at Melton for the hunting. I spend pots of money on my clothes, and I need no man to buy me jewelry, I thank you; I can buy my own. Although I must say that ruby bracelet Peyton gave you is exquisite, my dear Emma!"

"Yes, isn't it?" Madam Hart asked complacently. "The wages of sin, I fear, but *such* recompense." She extended her arm and admired the bracelet in question. "That was to celebrate my triumph in *Twelfth Night*," she recalled mistily. "Peyton is such a generous man, I can't help but adore him, you know."

"But if Peyton were to start telling you how to play your roles, you would resent it deeply, wouldn't you?" Audrey asked.

"Peyton would never dare! I am the premiere diva

of the English stage!" Madam Hart announced nonchalantly.

"My point exactly! Emma dear, don't you see? I have the perfect life. I enjoy robust health, have more money than I could ever spend in my life, lovely houses which I run to suit myself, wonderful friends like you, a very full social schedule (too full, what with all these peace parades and balls and rout parties and fireworks displays and whatnot!) and my blissful independence! My life is perfect just as it is!"

Madam Hart looked about the phaeton for a piece of wood to rap with her knuckles. "Oh, my dear, I wish you had not said that!" Like most theater people, she was extremely superstitious. "When you draw attention to your good fortune, you attract bad luck!"

"Nonsense!" Audrey replied briskly. "What could possibly go wrong?"

She would soon find out.

"Certainly, Major Shelby is a very handsome man," Miss Appolonia Fishbank said carefully. "A very handsome *young* man." If she stressed the *young* ever so slightly, Lady Wellford appeared to be too preoccupied with adjusting her earrings to notice. She glanced into the mirror at her former governess's reflection.

"He does quite take one's breath away, doesn't he, Appie?" she asked. "Do you think that I should have worn the sapphires instead? Would they go better with this gown?"

"No, I think your rose diamonds are quite appropriate," Miss Fishbank replied. "Audrey, my dear, you know that I hesitate to thrust my opinions forward.

After all, you are an adult and a widow and a woman of substantial responsibility, past the age when you need a preceptoress, but—"

"He's too young for me." Audrey finished, turning to look at her companion. "Tell me this, Appie. Why did no one raise an eyebrow when Wellford, who was old enough to be my father, offered for me? And yet, when I see a man only a very few years younger than I, it is the latest on-dit in town? It is not unknown, you know. Besides, I don't look quite like a crone yet, do I?"

Miss Fishbank had to smile. "Of course not," she said. "But—"

Habits of easy and honest conversation had existed between the two women for so long that neither hesitated to express their opinions. That Miss Fishbank prefaced her opening sally with the thought that she never interfered would ordinarily be enough to make Audrey smile, since Appie never hesitated to give her opinion. That Audrey was guiltily aware that she did not follow Miss Fishbank's advice as often as she should also bore weight.

Miss Fishbank, who knew her former charge better than anyone, save perhaps the late Lord Wellford, understood Audrey very well. Beneath the glittering shell of a lady of fashion the unhappy child of Bleakfriars still cried out for love. Her own affection was tinged with gratitude. As soon as she was married, Audrey had persuaded her indulgent husband to allow her the company of her old governess. For saving her from the dismal and destitute retirement a former governess might have expected, Miss Fishbank would always be thankful. In the Wellford household, she was treated with every consideration, a circumstance most unusual for one in her position, as Appie was only too well aware. Brought up to earn her keep, she occupied herself by keeping Audrey's domestic arrangements running smoothly. In spite of her former mentor's best efforts, Audrey had no interest in household management.

Gratitude, however, was not enough to still her tongue. A vicar's daughter, a female of high principles herself, she often deplored Audrey's more outrageous escapades, and once or twice had even threatened to remove herself from the household in the wake of some particularly reprehensible adventure. But in the end, she always stayed on. "If I departed, you would lose what few shreds of respectability you have left," she would sniff.

Even Audrey had to acknowledge the truth of that. Besides, as exasperating as her dear Miss Fishbank could be, with her stern opinions about manners and morals, Audrey knew she would be quite lost without her dear Appie.

With this thought in mind, she turned in a rustle of silk and impulsively hugged the spinster. "Poor Appie! Please don't worry. If you do, it shall drive me mad, you know."

Miss Fishbank returned the embrace. "I only wish that—well, it doesn't matter what I wish for! You would look very fetching, my dear, if you would pull your décolletage just a little!" As she spoke, she suited her actions to her words, and a bit less of Lady Wellford was exposed.

Audrey laughed, but made no attempt to restore her neckline to its former level. A last critical glance at herself in the mirror showed a handsome woman attired in a deep rose dinner dress of watered silk, the corsage and hem trimmed in lozenges of ivory crepe caught with silver lamé ribbons. Her dark hair was styled *à la Cupide* and held in place with an ivory comb, and there was just a hint of rouge on her cheeks. On her feet, she wore embroidered slippers of white on ivory kid. The rose diamonds at her throat and ears set off the sparkle in her gray eyes, rimmed with thick, dark lashes. She smelled faintly and deliciously of jasmine. In short, she was the very picture of a lady of fashion.

As she patted a curl into place, Wescott, her abigail, opened the door, bearing a spangled shawl of deep claret, which she draped over Lady Wellford's elbow. "Major Shelby is downstairs, my lady," she said after giving her mistress a critical appraisal and adjusting the errant curl to her satisfaction. Highly fashionable and hideously expensive, she would not allow a lady in her charge to appear in public looking anything less than perfect. In this respect, Lady Wellford and Wescott were well suited.

"Don't wait up for me," Audrey commanded. "I daresay I shall not be in until quite late, and I shall want to sleep in tomorrow morning, so there's no need to wake me up before ten."

Appie clucked disapprovingly, but said nothing as Audrey gathered up her skirts and departed from the dressing room.

At the top of the stairs, she took a deep breath and slowly descended the risers, making one of her famous entrances.

Major Shelby, at the foot of the staircase, was a most appreciative audience. He gazed upward with such an expression of adoration on his countenance that Otterbine, the butler, had to suppress a cough behind his hand. More handsome than ever in his dress hussar uniform, the major bowed and offered his arm. "You will be the most beautiful woman present tonight," he promised. "Everyone will envy me."

"Thank you, Giles. Since we are dining at Carlton House, I shall at least be the youngest woman present, I daresay. The Prince Regent likes his women matronly! But I heard that Wellington himself is expected to be there tonight! Thank you, Otterbine, please don't wait up for me. I expect to be quite late coming in."

Otterbine bowed his employer and her escort out of the door.

"Her ladyship's going to dinner where the Duke of Wellington will be tonight!" he loftily informed the footman, who was suitably awed by the mention of the hero of Salamanca.

It seemed that all of London had gone mad in the wake of the peace celebrations. The streets were draped in bunting and Union Jacks, and there were fireworks almost every night. All the heroes of the endless wars were in town, including no less a personage of note than the Russian Tsar. Nothing would do for London's hostesses but to vie with each other in a series of dinners, balls, and parties to celebrate the visits of so many famous people. Every day, the stack of invitations on Audrey's mantel grew thicker, and she was hard pressed to recall the last time she had spent an evening at home by the fire.

It was very agreeable to her to be out and about, and very agreeable to her to be seen on the arm of a handsome young war hero at this ball or that party. If the unkind thought sometimes intruded that Major Shelby might be less interesting if he were less handsome and less a hero of the hour, she was able to suppress it without a qualm. Since the death of her husband, she had enjoyed a string of flirtations of varying length and depth. While her widowhood had been by no means cloistered, her heart was never seriously engaged. And yet, in spite of herself, she sometimes felt a desire to be settled. Whether or not Major Shelby was the man with whom she wished to be settled, she was unsure. But in the coach, stealing a sideways glance at his burnished curls as he held her hand and spoke animatedly about some subject she was not quite listening to, she wondered if she might not grant him the surrender he sought.

He was, after all, so very handsome. And she was, after all, a woman, with all the desires of a woman. Provided, of course, that the liaison could be accomplished discreetly. Practice had made Audrey very adept at discretion; Miss Fishbank had a sharp eye.

Impulsively, she leaned over and placed her lips upon those of Giles Shelby, who responded with an enthusiasm that took her breath away. Alas, he also made her aware that he was crumpling her dress.

"Oh, my dearest Audrey, my love!" he exclaimed. "That you could grant me—my dearest love."

"*After the dinner.* I have a side entrance into my house. No one will see us. I told everyone that they were not to wait up for me tonight," Audrey said, moving away slightly so that she could spread out her skirts.

Giles responded enthusiastically, and Audrey finally had to gently disengage his embrace. "You're disarranging my hair, Giles! Do you want to arrive at Carlton House looking as if we'd been trysting in the coach?" In spite of herself, she was laughing. Giles's very passions were like those of an affectionate puppy. For a lady who was used to more sophisticated admirers, the novelty was its own excitement.

"I don't care who knows it!" Giles declared passionately. "I could let down the window and let all of London know!" Giles threw himself into setting his actions to words with all the fire of impetuous youth. Audrey quickly restrained him.

Giles fell back against the seat. "You have made me the happiest man in London," he said. "Of course, when my mother and my sisters come to town, you will want to meet them—"

Audrey raised an eyebrow. "I hardly think—" she began.

But Giles rushed on, oblivious. "After all, now that you have agreed to marry me, there can be no—but would you prefer to wait for the wedding?"

"The wedding?"

"I asked if you would marry me, and in response you kissed me, my dearest. Surely that is an assent. I realize that since you have been married before, you have no missish qualms about er, intimacy, but if you prefer to wait for the wedding before we consummate our love, I will try my best to wait, although—"

Audrey made a mental note that in future she must listen more closely when Giles talked. *If only he did not seem to talk a great deal of romantic nonsense,* she thought, just a little irritated. Unfortunately, Giles was at his most appealing when he was also at his most boyishly enthusiastic. His eyes sparkled, his perfect white teeth shone forth in a disarming smile; even the cleft in his well-defined chin seemed a little deeper. When he smiled, as he was doing now, he was irresistible.

"Marriage was not uppermost in my thoughts when

I kissed you, Giles," she confessed, however, determined to stay on the point.

"The next few hours will crawl past for me," he said, kissing her hand.

At that moment, the coach rumbled to a stop. The door was thrown open and the steps let down by a footman in the Prince Regent's red and gold livery. No further conversation was possible as Lady Wellford adjusted her hair and climbed down from the coach, hoping very much that the color in her cheeks was not too high.

Carlton House was ablaze with light. Although the Regent's flagrant scandals had placed him quite beyond the pale with the highest sticklers, his position prevented even his most disdainful critics from refusing an invitation to one of his evenings. Lady Wellford, of course, had few scruples and less regard for gossip. Had she been thirty years older, she might have become a member of the Carlton House Set. Even so, she found most of the Prince's scandals rather sophomoric, if not downright dull.

Still, no one would have missed this chance to be in the same room with the Duke of Wellington. As Lady Wellford and Major Shelby were ushered through a phalanx of footmen into the Gold Salon, Audrey noted many, many familiar faces in the crowd. Sir Peyton Rudge, resplendent in evening dress with a great many fobs and seals and an enormous ruby thrust into his neckcloth, appeared at Audrey's side.

"Gad, what a crush, hey?" he asked without preamble, nodding distantly at Giles. "Looks like everyone is here tonight. Pity Prinny's got a bee in his bonnet about night air. If it gets any hotter in here, you may be sure that some of the ladies will start to faint. Ah, well, it makes no mind. Come along and pay your respects to Prinny and the Duke before the dinner bell sounds. Prinny's anxious to meet you, Shelby! The Duke speaks well of you! Afterwards we may all be comfortable with a rubber or two of whist. Got to give me a chance to win back those five hundred guineas I lost to you last week, don't you know. Pity Emma couldn't be here."

"Yes, it is." Both of them accepted without question that an actress would never be invited into a gathering such as this. It was simply the way of their world.

The Prince Regent swept a low bow over Lady Wellford's hand. His stays creaked audibly. "I know that the evening will be a complete success whenever I see you in the throng," he said genially. Abysmal failure though he might be considered as a prince, a son, a husband, a father, and a friend, Audrey was always amazed by his enormous, all-encompassing charm. When he smiled and asked interestedly after her matched grays and her new high perch phaeton, it was easy to see how her father's generation could have considered him the first gentleman of Europe. Encased in his evening coat like a sausage in a skin, his several chins cascading over his unfortunate choice of a neckcloth, his face a map of years of excesses and indulgences, there were still traces of handsome Prince Florizel in his eyes.

Like many another of his subjects, Audrey found herself, in spite of all, warming to his peculiar gift, his pervasive charm.

His Royal Highness's affability extended to Major Shelby also; he exclaimed over the bravery of the

young soldier and expressed a wish that he might have
been there to join in the fray. The Regent graciously
complimented him upon being such a lucky dog as to
escort such a beauty as Lady Wellford, welcomed
them both to make free of his hospitality and passed
them on to the Duke of Wellington still basking in
the glow of his charisma. It was all done so smoothly
that not even Audrey noticed that they had been
dismissed, even as the Prince turned his attention to
the next people in the reception line.

The Iron Duke, Audrey noticed as she shook his
thin, limp fingers, had no such charm. If anything, his
long, aquiline face had the look of a man enduring
inescapable boredom, and he spoke in fragmented
sentences. "Rather. Yes, Lady Wellford. An honor."
At the sight of young Major Shelby, he relaxed
slightly—but only slightly. "Make the most of it,
m'boy, and never miss a chance to sit down or relieve
yourself. Damned long evening, what? Makes a man
yearn for the field and the camp!"

"Very high accolades indeed! You seem to have
scored another conquest!" Giles crowed to Audrey as
soon as they had left the receiving line and were free
to wander through the vast, overdecorated halls of
Carlton House, gawking, like the rest of the crowd, at
the gilt and sphinx-headed excesses of the Regent's
taste as represented in his London residence. Giles
grasped two glasses of champagne from a passing
footman and handed one to Audrey, who sipped
gratefully. "I told you Old Hook would be mad for
you."

"Yes, the Duke positively *exuded* enthusiasm,"
Audrey said dryly.

"I don't know why everyone says the Regent is so

Gothic," Giles continued. "Why, he seems very kind, said everything that was civil to me. That is something m'mother and sisters will want to hear about, me meeting the Regent."

"Oh, very civil," Audrey replied. She noticed, as he never did, that a number of ladies were staring at him with something approaching adoration. Giles, the least vain of men, was oblivious to the effect of his looks. Audrey, however, felt a definite sense of satisfaction that she was in the company of an Adonis. She quickly gathered her thoughts, remembering her vow to listen to what the major said, however inconsequential. "He can be, you know, if he isn't foxed, and you haven't crossed him, or you aren't related to him, or he doesn't owe you money from whist, or—"

"Audrey, he *is* the Prince Regent!" Giles said a little reprovingly. Audrey felt a stab of annoyance at his tone, and she looked at him in a way that would have warned any one of her friends that they had gone too far. Lady Wellford was not one to take criticism kindly, however well meant. Giles's attempts to impose his standards upon her could be excessively trying, since she felt she knew a great deal more about the ways of the fashionable world than a young soldier from a provincial town in the Cotswolds. A biting remark was on the tip of her tongue when Giles, sensing something amiss, looked down at her face.

"Oh, my dearest Audrey!" he exclaimed, instantly apologetic. "Forgive me, but you must admit, my dearest, that is no respectful way to speak of a Prince of the Realm."

"When Prinny does something to deserve my respect, I am sure that I will not be behind in paying it to him." Audrey snapped her fan open and aired herself vigorously.

The room was intensely close; because of the Regent's dislike of fresh air, the windows remained tightly closed. She felt a thin beading of perspiration on her forehead, and downed the rest of her glass of champagne.

She had the sudden sensation that she was being observed. Since this was in no way unusual for her, she glanced around to see what gossiping tongue was wagging, but instead she found herself looking into the face of a dark-haired, deeply tanned gentleman across the room.

He smiled and lifted his glass in her direction in what she could only deplore as a most encroaching fashion.

"Giles, who is that man?" she asked. "That dark man across the room, the one who is staring and smiling at me?"

Giles looked in the direction she indicated. "It's that same fellow we saw in the park, ain't it? The one with the big black gelding?" he asked. "By gad, there he is again. Shall I give him a set-down for staring at you so?"

Audrey shook her head. "Show a little restraint, Giles, if you please! He *looks* so familiar, but I can't recall how or where. How extremely odd, to be sure."

"Here comes Sylvia Godolphin," Giles said gloomily as that lady bore relentlessly down upon them.

"Quick, let's go the other way. I think I see Sally Jersey in the next room," Audrey said, the dark man completely forgotten.

At that moment, the gong sounded for dinner, and they were lost in the general rush to find their places in precedence.

*   *   *

The sleepy watchman was calling the hour of two, and the house on Half Moon Street was illuminated only by a few dimmed gaslights as Major Shelby opened the wrought iron gate. Audrey and Giles giddily tiptoed through the side passageway.

"Seventeen courses and twenty different wines," Audrey sighed, leaning against the Major's broad shoulder. "I am quite as foxed on food as champagne. Soup, fish, chicken, grouse, beef, lobster, lamb, venison, oysters, cheese, sorbet, *and* a bombe richelieu. And who knows how many removes and side dishes? Hock, claret, Madeira—"

"Shh, my dearest! You'll wake the whole house. I thought the evening would *never* end. But here we are, alone at last. Are you sure your woman won't wait up for you?"

"Wescott is sublimely indifferent to my comings and goings—why can't I get this key to fit in this lock? This is my house and my side door. I just open it up, and we sneak up the stairs, and we're in my boudoir and no one the wiser—" Audrey frowned as she tried to fix the key to the lock with some difficulty.

"The wines *were* too numerous at dinner," Giles said. "I think we may both be just a trifle foxed, my dearest."

"Nonsense, I have a head as hard as a rock! I am never foxed," Audrey declared passionately, if a bit unsteadily. She paused to kiss the major long and hard.

"Not here, upstairs," she said when his response threatened to overwhelm her. "Mmm, Giles, that's enough. I've got to get this *damned* door opened or we'll be out here all night."

The major's response was to draw her closer against himself in order to deliver to her a soul-stirring kiss.

"Upstairs—" Lady Wellford tried to say. There was, she thought, nothing quite so exciting as the very beginning of an affair.

The key finally turned in the lock, but not by Audrey's hand.

Light spilled from the opened doorway, and Otterbine, a candelabra in his hand suddenly appeared. Trained in the old school and a professional to the core, not by so much as a raised eyebrow did he betray the least surprise at the sight of his employer in an embrace with her handsome beau.

The fact of the matter was, greater things were occupying his mind.

"Thank goodness you're home, my lady," he said. "Miss Fishbank thought we ought not to send the second footman after you. After all, it is Carlton House. But we are all quite at a loss as to what to do."

"Is that her, Otterbine? Audrey, you must come at once. She quite refuses to budge until she has spoken to you, and I am not at all sure what to do." Miss Fishbank's figure appeared behind that of the butler. The two of them, Audrey noted rather dully, were in their nightclothes.

She only had time to disengage herself from Giles' embrace before Appie adjusted her spectacles and got a good look at the major, who had the grace to blush a deep crimson. "Just making sure Lady Wellford came home safely," he murmured.

"What in the world is going on?" Audrey asked, summoning as much dignity as she could muster, given the circumstances. "I thought I asked you not to wait up for me."

"We were all abed, like decent people should be," Miss Fishbank said, with a speaking look at the major, "when there was this terrible loud knocking at the door. Of course, my first thought was bad news, one always thinks that so late at night, but Audrey, I really felt I had no choice. After all, one can't put the girl out on the streets—"

"What girl? Appie, you know I have no interest in the peccadilloes of the maids—"

"It is not one of the maids, Audrey."

"It's a Young Person," Otterbine added. "She refused to go away. Insisted she had to see you, my lady."

"What Young Person?" Audrey asked, her head swimming as much with confusion as wine.

"She *says* she is your niece," Otterbine said with a hint of disapproval in his voice.

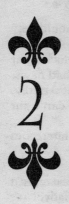

2

"*Niece? Do I have any* nieces, Appie?*" Lady Wellford appealed to her companion. "If I do, they ought to be at Bleakfriars in the schoolroom, not jaunting about London at all hours of the day and night. A fine thing, to let a child go jaunting all over London. Is her maid with her?"

"The Young Person only has a bandbox," Otterbine said ominously.

"But, Audrey, she's not—"

"I comprehend it all now!" Lady Wellford laughed, rather pleased with herself. "This must be Emma Hart's idea of a little joke. Although I must say her timing could not be worse—doubtless some ingenue from the theater—"

"Audrey, I don't—" Miss Fishbank started to say, then closed her lips firmly. She looked at Major Shelby with frank disapproval, and Giles had the grace to blush.

"I placed the Young Person in the Green Salon, my lady," Otterbine said.

"Audrey, she's not an—" Miss Fishbank started to say, but Audrey, highly amused, had plunged into the Green Salon.

"Now, see here, young lady, I don't know how much Emma paid you to play this joke, but—" Audrey's words died on her lips.

A young girl of perhaps seventeen summers sat forlornly amidst the grandeur of nile green brocade and gilt sphinx-headed couches. The elegant formality of the room contrasted sharply with her rumpled aspect. She wore a plain scoop bonnet and a wrinkled pelisse of a decidedly drab and unfashionable cut. The bandbox that had caused Otterbine so much pain lay at her feet. As she rose tremulously to her feet, she twisted a dingy handkerchief between her fingers. Audrey stopped in her tracks, for once in her life speechless.

This was no actress, but a properly-brought-up schoolroom miss. No actress would be caught dead in such a dowdy pelisse.

"A-Aunt Audrey?" the girl asked in a small frightened voice. Tears spilled from her eyes. "Oh, it must be you! I would know you anywhere!" Without further ado, the girl threw herself into Audrey's arms, sobbing as if her heart would break. "I am your niece, Susan," she cried. "Please don't send me back! I would rather die than go back there!"

Automatically, Audrey turned her eyes toward Miss Fishbank, pleading for help.

"Your brother's oldest girl," Appie murmured

helpfully. From her reticule, she produced a clean handkerchief, which she handed to the girl. "Susan Dysart."

Audrey racked her memory. She was dimly aware that her brother and That Woman had offspring, but she was not aware that any of them were *quite* so grown-up.

"Forgive me, my dear, but I have allowed a thick, dark fog to descend between me and anything to do with my brother and sister-in-law," she said frankly. "You are Robert's daughter?"

"Y-yes. I am Susan. And there are Frank and Barney at home. Except Frank is at Oxford," she added, oblivious to Audrey's wince at this news.

"Yes, of course, your father is years and years older than I," Audrey said quickly, avoiding Miss Fishbank's eye. "But what are you doing here? How did you get here?"

These questions triggered a fresh outpouring of tears, and overwhelmed, Miss Dysart sank into the sofa again. "Oh, please, do not send me back there! I would sooner die!"

"There's no need to make a watering pot of yourself," Audrey said, not unkindly. "Otterbine, be good enough to fetch us a pot of strong tea and some food," she ordered crisply. "I daresay it would do us all some good. And," she added, with heavy meaning in her tone, "I trust you will be discreet about this episode."

Otterbine looked affronted, but dutifully marched away to the nether regions.

Audrey turned her attention back to the girl. "I assume you have run away from home," she said.

"Yes. I *had* to, you see!" Susan turned a stained

face to her aunt. "I can't marry him, you see!"

Audrey's hands clenched and unclenched, and her expression took on a steely cast. "I begin to see how it is—again!" she exclaimed fiercely. "Your parents are forcing you to marry someone you cannot abide, is that it?"

"Audrey—" Miss Fishbank said cautiously. But Audrey was not to be restrained.

"Damn Robert! And That Woman, too! Was there ever a bigger pair of greedy fools?" Audrey raged.

Susan shrank from her. "I am sorry, Aunt Audrey. I . . . I . . . oh!" Fresh torrents poured forth.

Nervously, Audrey patted her shoulder. "There, there, I did not mean you to think I am angry with you! Angry *for* you, yes! Tell me how you came here!"

"I-I could not go to Grandmama Eppington in Bath, for she would be ever so angry and tell me that I must do my d-duty by Papa and Mama, so I came here. I had some money put by, and Barney, my younger brother, gave me what he had. He would have come, but there wasn't enough to pay for both our passages on the mail coach, so I came alone!" As she spoke, she blew her nose into Appie's clean handkerchief. "Papa had locked me in my room and Mama was so angry—but Barney found the key and let me out and I sneaked away in the middle of the night and caught the London Mail at Hand Cross." She wiped away tears.

Audrey laughed. "Well, that shows more spirit than I had! I wish I had thought of such a thing when I was placed in your situation."

"Audrey!" Miss Fishbank cautioned her again.

"Barney and I *thought* that you would understand.

I would have written to you, but there was no time, it all happened so swiftly, and then Papa locked me in my room and I couldn't write to anyone. But I cannot marry him! I would rather die first!"

Sensing that yet more tears were forthcoming, Audrey quickly said, "Please, my dear! If you make a watering pot out of yourself, nothing can be accomplished! Am I to understand that your father and That Woman—I mean your mother—wanted to you to marry against your will? So much so that they locked you in your room until you consented?"

Susan nodded vigorously. "You can't imagine what it's like to be browbeaten and bullied and threatened. Mama said it was my duty to marry Lord Merlin!"

"Merlin? Good Lord, he must be all of eighty!"

"He is very, very old," Susan agreed. "And he terrifies me! But if I marry him, he will pay all of Papa's debts, although I do not understand precisely how. Mama says it is my Duty!"

"Duty? Duty to marry that old man? Why, Merlin's old enough to be your great-grandfather, and quite senile in the bargain! Besides being a lifelong bachelor, if you know what I mean, no, dear, never mind, you probably do not know what I mean, save that the entire thing is quite mad and would never do! What in the world did Robert do with the money Wellford settled on me, I'd like to know. No, I don't want to know! Odious! Oh, I can see my dear brother and That Woman scheming and plotting this, just as they did with Wellford and me!" Agitated, Audrey rose from the sofa and paced the room. "I don't know what to do; I must think," she said at last. "But one thing is clear; I cannot put you out on the street! Dear Lord, the public stagecoach! You see, Appie, this is what my brother has wrought, him and That Woman!"

"Audrey, my dear, you must gain control over yourself," Miss Fishbank said. "Giving way to your passions never serves!"

Otterbine, returning with a tray, cleared his throat. "I could prepare the Blue Chamber for the Young Lady, ma'am," he said. "I thought you might prefer that the upstairs maid not be awakened."

"Thank you, Otterbine. I knew I could count upon you," Miss Fishbank said gratefully, which somewhat mollified that superior servant's ruffled feelings. He placed the tray on the table and bowed.

"If you like, I shall inform the other servants that the Young Lady was detained in town by an accident to her carriage and naturally sought out her aunt's home in the emergency. That should quell any unfortunate speculation belowstairs."

"Otterbine, you are a complete hand," Audrey said. "I don't know what I would do without you."

The august butler allowed himself a small smile. "You may leave it all to me," he assured her, bearing Miss Dysart's battered bandbox away with him.

"For heaven's sake, child, take off that awful bonnet," Audrey commanded her niece.

Susan undid her bonnet strings. "You won't throw me out?" she asked. Without the hideous bonnet, she was revealed to have dark hair and blue, albeit red-rimmed, eyes. There was a definite Dysart resemblance between aunt and niece.

"Don't be silly, eat something," Audrey commanded. "You are quite safe here with Miss Fishbank and me."

Giles, who had been hanging uncertainly at the doorway watching this scene, cleared his throat.

"Perhaps I ought to take my leave now," he suggested uncertainly.

Audrey looked up. "Giles! I am excessively sorry! I had forgotten all about you! Major Shelby, allow me to make you known to my niece, Susan Dysart."

"How do you do?" she asked shyly. Unlike most women first beholding the major's extraordinary looks, her attention wavered toward the tray of food on the table before her.

"Nice to meet you," the major said, too well-bred to allow his resentment of her sudden intrusion into his evening's plans to show.

"I shall see you to the door," Audrey said. "Appie, make the child eat something."

"Giles, I am so sorry about all of this," she said in the deserted hallway. "I had no idea—"

The major sighed. "It cannot be helped, but what timing the chit has!" he murmured petulantly. "Dearest Audrey, I yearn for you. I want you, I burn for you—" He swept her into his arms.

"Yes, yes, and I for you, also," Audrey said briskly, disengaging herself from his embrace. "But not in the hallway at three in the morning, I thank you! Go home and get a night's sleep, Giles. I'll speak to you tomorrow."

"Sleep! How can I sleep when I want you so much?" Giles moaned. "Audrey, please!"

"Well then, go home and read a good book. Giles! I have enough to deal with right now," she pleaded, suddenly very tired.

"Very well," Giles said reluctantly.

"So kind, my dear, do call tomorrow—" She eased him out the door before he could demand another kiss and closed it firmly behind him.

The sight of food had cheered Susan immensely. She needed no second invitation to help herself to cold chicken, bread, cheese, and fruit. "There was no time to eat on the road. By the time they served the food at the inn, the coachman was sounding his horn again." She ate ravenously as Miss Fishbank poured cups of strong tea. "When we reached London, I only had enough for a hansom cab to bring me here," she was telling Miss Fishbank.

"It is not pleasant to use public transportation," that lady agreed. "So crowded, so dirty and uncertain. In my days as a governess, I was forced to depend upon it."

Susan nodded. "This is the first time I have ever been to London. It's the first time I've been anywhere other than Bath, really."

"How came you to meet Merlin?" Audrey asked, seating herself wearily in a chair and accepting a cup of tea. Idly she began to remove her jewelry, dropping it carelessly on a table.

Susan's chin trembled dangerously at the mention of Lord Merlin, but she was distracted by the glittering pile Audrey had cast so carelessly aside. It was outside her experience to see valuables treated so recklessly.

"He was in Bath, and he happened to see me at one of the Assemblies with Mama. Oh, he is old, and so—vague! I am so afraid of him!"

"Merlin always was strange," Audrey agreed, ready to work herself into a fine anger against her brother and sister-in-law again. "The entire family is like that, the odd manners, you know!" Audrey sipped at her tea, thinking. "That Woman must have been mad to think of making a match for you with that lot."

"Audrey, my dear!" Appie cautioned her.

But Audrey was not to be stopped. "Well, it's true, you know! Appie, I defy you to think of anything so Gothic! Every sense is outraged! Marrying a girl not yet out of the schoolroom to Merlin!"

"He doesn't love me, he said he didn't," Susan continued gloomily. "He said that he must be married and produce an heir and that I would do as well as the next girl. That I would soon learn to respect him, and that he would mold me to be Lady Merlin. But I don't *want* to be Lady Merlin!"

"Infamous! He must be senile!" Audrey exclaimed. "Tell me, Susan, is there someone else?"

Her niece shook her head. "No, no one. After Merlin offered for me, Mama took me back to Bleakfriars immediately. And that was my Season," she said in a small voice. She looked from Appie to Audrey with her huge gray eyes. "Don't you see? I *had* to run away! I can't marry him! Please don't send me back there!" There was a hysterical edge to her voice and it looked at if she would cry again. "You were my only hope! Everyone knows about you, Aunt Audrey."

"No one is going to send you anywhere," Audrey said quickly. To forestall more tears, she patted Susan's arm.

"Now, I think we all ought to get some sleep," Miss Fishbank said. "Tomorrow, we can sort this all out."

Audrey leaned back in her chair and closed her eyes. "Lord, what a night!" she sighed.

A single cheery sunbeam penetrated the window hangings. It stole through a tiny chink in the gauze and the brocade curtains and fell across the pale Aubusson. It sparkled on the *famille verte* porcelain on the mantel and glittered on the silver lamp on the table. Slowly, as Half Moon Street came alive, it penetrated into a corner of the room where a very fine Vigée-Lebrun portrait, rescued from the French Revolution by the late Lord Wellford, hung against the hand-painted wallpaper, looking down with faint disapproval at the sleeper in the elaborately carved and ormolued bed. The sunbeam, as it rose, cast a long thin beam across the recumbent form nestled among the lace and linen and pillows.

Moving on soundless feet, Wescott entered the room. She cast a disapproving look at the clock on the rosewood escritoire, then at the slumbering figure in the bed. In her hand, she held the heap of jewels so carelessly left on a table the night before. She crossed the room to a japanned cabinet, which she opened with a key, and scrupulously laid the rose diamond parure, piece by piece, in its own velvet-lined drawer, which she carefully closed. She then locked the japanned cabinet again, clucking her tongue all the while.

Crossing to the windows, Wescott drew back the curtains with a gesture an observer might have called vehement. The midmorning sunlight of a fine London day poured into the room.

"Good morning, my lady," Wescott said, just a fraction louder than she needed to.

The figure in the bed moaned, pulled a pillow over her head and rolled deeper into the featherbed.

"Wescott, I am going to *sack* you," a voice said from somewhere deep in the lace and ruffles.

"I have a pot of coffee ready for you," the abigail said matter-of-factly. "The girl is coming up with your bathwater." Wescott paused a beat. "I have taken the liberty of unpacking the Young Lady's bandbox," she added. Unspoken but sensed was that the contents of the bandbox would never do.

From deep within her pounding head, the whole of the previous evening rose up in all its glory to Audrey's emerging consciousness. She groaned. "Go away. I don't want to *think* right now."

"A bit of hartshorn and water on your temples will make you feel much better," Wescott said. She went into the dressing room and returned with the bottle. "It always does."

From a great depth, Audrey swam to the surface. Her head throbbed, her mouth felt as if it were stuffed with rags, and her neck ached. *I'm getting too old for this,* she thought, and promptly put the thought out of her head. "The wines," she said with a vast dignity she was far from feeling, "were too numerous."

Wescott said nothing, but poured hot, thick coffee from a silver pot. Audrey took the cup from her gratefully. The coffee revived her a little, and the cool cloth, soaked with hartshorn, that the abigail placed on her forehead soothed her aching skull. While the tweeny filled the shell-shaped tub in the dressing room, Wescott massaged her mistress's temples.

"A protracted soak in hot water might make me feel as if I could face the rest of the day, if not the rest of my life," Audrey sighed. She was quite used to having every attention lavished on her. What was the good of having a sizable fortune if not to be able to command endless amounts of coddling for oneself? she frequently asked.

Left to soak in the deliciously hot water, perfumed with her favorite otto of roses, Audrey snuggled down into the tub and closed her eyes, preparing for a long, luxurious meditation on the sensual pleasures of doing *exactly* as one pleased, which, after all, she told herself, was the great point of being a well-to-do widow with no responsibilities other than to please herself. And one of the ways in which she could please herself was to enjoy a protracted bath, dreaming in the warm water until she turned wrinkled and waterlogged. Such luxuries had been frowned upon at Bleakfriars, where hot water and fires in the bedrooms had been considered unnecessary luxuries of considerable expense. Naturally, upon marriage, Audrey had taken to long, hot baths and fires in the bedchamber with a passion.

Lifting one foot to the edge of the shell-shaped tub, she studied her gilded toenail with satisfaction and relaxed with a sigh, allowing herself to go limp. Once a week, Wescott covered each toenail with gold leaf. Idly, she reached for the coffee tray and took a sip of coffee. Her head was feeling much better, she decided. Perhaps she was feeling just enough the thing to have a bite of toast and a little piece of fruit. She reached out for the tray and located, without looking, a bunch of grapes. She peeled one off the stem and popped it into her mouth, lost in bliss.

She was barely, just barely, beginning to feel human again. . . .

"Good morning, Aunt!" A cheerful, rather too cheerful voice sundered Lady Wellford's peace. With a jerk, Audrey sat bolt upright, scattering grapes everywhere.

Susan appeared in the doorway, attired in a sprigged muslin dress. Her smile quavered a bit as she regarded her aunt. It was not so much that she had startled Lady Wellford as the sight of her sybaritic bathtub and her gilded toenails. Susan's eyes grew very wide indeed.

"Oh, I am sorry! I did not mean to disturb you! Should I come back?"

Audrey slowly sat up. Dim memories of the previous evening were beginning to rise in her consciousness.

Niece. What was her name? Ran away from Bleakfriars and her dreadful brother. No wonder. Steady now, Audrey, you can cope with this. Like a very dim light at the end of a very long tunnel, enlightenment began to flood through Audrey's somewhat dazed consciousness. *Good Lord,* Audrey thought, *do I really have a niece who's almost a woman?*

Swiftly veering away from the direction *that* thought would take, Audrey smiled, feeling as if her face would crack. "Ah, *Susan!* What an unexpected treat and so early in the morning, too. Would you please hand me that towel on the rack?"

Susan did as she was bid, "I'm very sorry! I didn't mean to burst in on you in your bath. Shall I come back? It was just that the noise woke me up and I couldn't get back to sleep. London is so full of sound, you know. Coaches and street vendors and people. Does anyone ever sleep here?"

Audrey lifted herself from her bath and dried herself with the towel. "Sometimes I think not," she smiled. "The Metropolis is a very busy place, you know."

"I saw a little of it last night, but it was dark. Aunt, do ladies of fashion all paint their toenails with gold?"

Audrey, engaged in wrapping herself into a peignoir of violet shot silk, unconsciously curled her toes. "Only the most dashing of them," she replied swiftly. To forestall further questions along those lines,

Audrey sat down at her dressing table and pushed her feet into a pair of embroidered satin mules.

Susan circled the room, taking in the green and white striped wallpaper, the ornately carved marble mantelpiece, the India muslin crewel-worked curtains, the Aubusson rugs, the ormolu clock on the little table, the gold-capped crystal vials spread across the dressing table. She stopped to glance through the open door of Audrey's bedchamber and stared in wonder at the large curtained bed, the Vigée-Lebrun portrait, the rose damask hangings. "You have fires in every room!" she exclaimed. "I have never been in a house that was so boilingly, wonderfully warm before!"

Recalling the bone-chilling cold of Bleakfriars, Audrey shivered. "I cannot bear to be cold," she said with a little laugh. "When I was first married, I couldn't believe that Wellford—your late uncle— caused a great coal fire to be kindled in whatever room he happened to be in! What a luxury it seemed after huddling around that piddly little flame in the Hall at Bleakfriars. I trust your father still feels the cold is nice and bracing?" She tried to keep her tone even, but even so, a note of contempt crept into her voice.

"Oh yes!" Susan said, peering at a pair of K'ang-hsi figurines on a shelf. "Look at your books! *Mansfield Park!* How I have yearned to read that. But Mama says that novels are not improving! I—" A sudden cloud crossed her face and she turned to Audrey with a doleful look. "You won't send me back, will you? At least not for a while, if you please? I can't marry him, Aunt, I can't! He's so old and he terrifies me! He's so—overbearing! "

Audrey studied her niece for a moment, and saw in her face all the unforgotten misery of her own youth. She looked, at the first time, at Susan's shabby round gown. The sprigged muslin had been turned once, at least, she noted with distaste. Really, she would not be an unattractive girl if she had a proper haircut and some decent clothes and less of the look of a puppy about to be kicked. Something in her heart that had not been touched in many years stirred. It frightened her a little, who prided herself on her cynical character, and she frowned. "We'll see," she said. "But not until we have had a chance to talk it all over. Have you eaten your breakfast?"

Susan shook her head. She peered at her aunt hopefully.

"Well, first things first. It is obvious that you and I have a great deal of ground to cover, but not, I think, before you have some food."

In due course, breakfast was brought to Audrey's dressing room on a tray, and that lady watched with awe as her niece consumed a great quantity of scrambled eggs, kippers, bacon, toast, muffins and marmalade, washed down with several cups of milky tea. For such a small girl, she had a prodigious appetite. But then, as she explained disingenuously, for the past week she had been confined to her room on bread and water. "Papa and Mama were determined that I would come around in the end, you see. But I didn't! Instead I climbed out the window and took Frank and Barney's money and caught the London Mail at Hand Cross."

"My brother has not changed, I see. No doubt, with That Woman to encourage him on, he has reached a new level of tyranny!" Audrey exclaimed. Had Miss Fishbank been there to restrain her, no doubt she would have been more tactful in speaking of Susan's parents. But Miss Fishbank was not there, and Audrey, never one to censor herself where her brother and That Woman were concerned, gave full vent to her feelings. "Was there ever anything more odious?" she exclaimed. "Why, Lord Merlin must be *ancient* by now, and he's senile in the bargain! Whatever did my dear brother have in mind when he accepted such an offer—no, don't tell me! Merlin's as rich as a nabob! Dearest Brother Robert and That Woman cannot resist the smell of money! It is a great deal too bad that they didn't have six or seven daughters and sisters that they could sell into marriage! Was there ever anything more odious and despicable! Say no more, I know exactly how it was! For I have experienced that 'persuasion' myself! I was fortunate in that no one could have been kinder or more generous than Wellford. Indeed, he rescued me from Bleakfriars. . . ." Having worked herself into the fine temper that only the mention of her brother and sister-in-law could achieve, she was quite an impressive sight. Her eyes glittered, her bosom heaved, and her expression took on a cast that would have warned those who knew her that she was about to embark upon one of her starts.

Susan was quite impressed. Her fashionable, sophisticated aunt had met all of her expectations and more. At Bleakfriars, displays of emotion were rigidly suppressed, as were joy and laughter. She stored away this interesting scene for future reference, having already decided that Aunt Audrey was not only living up to her legend, but exactly the sort of female she wanted to become.

In a passion, Audrey rose from the table and paced the room. "You do not have to tell me the means used to coerce you! I know them all too well!"

Susan watched her aunt with admiration. Sweeping the train of her peignoir across the rug, her hair wrapped in the towel, Audrey offered a very gratifying imitation of Mrs. Siddons at her best. For a romantic-minded girl nurtured in an emotionally desolate environment, this was immensely stimulating. "Please don't send me back!" Susan pleaded. "I won't go! I would sooner put a period to my existence than return to Bleakfriars!"

"Of course I won't send you back there! How could I? But what I am to do with you? Is there no relation who would take you in?"

"Only Grandmama Eddington in Bath, and she would send me right back to Mama," Susan said desolately.

"Is there some young man in the neighborhood, some beau?" Audrey asked hopefully.

Susan shook her head. "How could there be when I was never allowed to go to the Minton Assemblies or even a dance at a neighbor's home?"

"Didn't your mama bring you out?" Audrey asked, much shocked at this dereliction of maternal duty.

"She said we would be spared the cost if I would accept Lord Merlin's suit, and then *he* could present me at a Drawing Room and bear the expense of a court dress."

"Odious, miserly, shabby-genteel, *cheeseparing* woman," Audrey said angrily. "*Precisely* what one might have expected from a spouse of Robert's!"

Susan's eyes grew very wide to hear Mama and Papa so roundly abused.

Audrey, who was a great believer in not doing things by halves, found the idea of her brother and sister-in-law's parsimony so repulsive that she continued on quite freely in this vein for some time, indulging in some quite choice epithets.

"W-what is an ogress?" Susan asked when her aunt paused to take a breath.

"Your mother, dear. That Woman." Audrey replied evenly. She threw herself into the chaise and pointed toward the writing desk. "Fetch me a piece of paper. In general, I hate writing letters, but I think the time has come to compose one to your parents."

"Does that mean I am to stay with you?"

"Yes, I suppose it does," Audrey said, a little surprised at herself. "Yes, I think you should stay here."

"Dearest Aunt Audrey!" Susan, in a flurry of tears, threw herself at her aunt's feet. In a long and varied career, a great many men had thrown themselves at those gilded toenails but no women, and certainly never an adoring niece.

It was quite enough to inspire Lady Wellford to new heights. As if struck by lightning, she had an idea.

"I shall bring you out myself! Yes, I shall launch you upon the ton right here in London! If I can't find you a husband you may love, no none can!"

Susan's eyes welled up with tears. "Oh, Aunt! You are the most wonderful woman in the world! Thank you! Thank you!" She gripped Audrey's hands into her own and threw herself at her feet.

"There, there," Audrey said, not at all displeased. "Now go make yourself ready! The next thing we need to do is go shopping! You must be suitably attired to meet this husband we'll find!"

It seemed, at that golden moment, like such a wonderful idea.

*   *   *

"What a ghastly idea!" Miss Fishbank exclaimed in a horrified voice. "You? Bring out a debutante! *You?* My dear Audrey, have you run mad?" Her spectacles slid to the end of her nose, and her gros point slid from her nerveless fingers. "Audrey, you are no more fit to have charge of a young girl than—than Letty Lade!"

"I've never been the mistress of a highwayman, although I must admit, Jack Shepherd was a very handsome man—but that don't signify! Of course I can do it, Appie!" In the wave of a new enthusiasm, Audrey was not to be checked. "Besides, if I don't, who will? We can't send the chit back to Bleakfrairs to marry Lord Merlin! Good Lord, I wouldn't wish that on my worst enemy, let alone an innocent girl."

"An innocent girl. Precisely my point!" Miss Fishbank said baldly. "Although I must admit that forcing that child to marry a man in his dotage is cruel. But you, my dear, in the role of respectable matchmaking chaperone? I think not!"

"I'm not *that* far sunk below reproach! I have always been *discreet!*" Audrey said defensively.

"Almack's!" Miss Fishbank said in depressing accents.

Audrey frowned "Well, I will grant you that is dull. Orangeat and flat champagne and the whole thing smelling strongly of the schoolroom, but I suppose I can endure a few evenings—"

"Vouchers! Having spent all these years twitting Mrs. Drummond Burrell and the other Patronesses and horrifying them with your escapades, do you really think they would offer you vouchers now?"

Audrey looked just a little doubtful in spite of herself. No debutante could be successfully launched into the very highest levels of Polite Society without admission to Almack's Assembly Rooms. And admission was strictly overseen by its Patronesses, a set of rich and influential matrons Audrey had gone out of her way to avoid for many years.

"Well, Sally Jersey would help me," she offered, naming the only one she could claim as a friend. Not a good friend, more of an acquaintance, but that was at least something.

"That's one. You need two Patronesses' approval for admission."

"Princess Lieven?" Audrey asked hopefully and received a speaking look for her pains. "Well, that don't signify right now. Besides, it was such a little joke, she may have forgotten about it. We'll have to have a ball, of course, and there are so many different parties and parades and entertainments going on to celebrate the peace that I'm sure we won't be dull!"

"I don't like it," Miss Fishbank said. "For one thing, I know you and your fits and starts. And for another, I doubt if you could behave yourself like a respectable widow if your life depended on it."

"I'm not that far beyond the pale!" Audrey retorted. "I think that my niece will have no need to blush in my company, Appie. I can be quite respectable if I want to! I was *most* respectable when Wellford was alive! I never gave him cause to blush for my conduct!" Audrey's chin was thrust out and her dark eyes were stubborn.

It was on the tip of her former governess's tongue to say *Thank God Lord Wellford can't see you now!* But Miss Fishbank, who knew that look well, merely shook her head. "It will look excessively odd to people, you know. What will you say about Robert and his wife?"

"I shall write them such a letter as they will soon comply. They will have to put a good face on it. No one save us will ever know she ran away from home. Besides," Audrey said, grinning in triumph, "I can't send her back, you know!"

"Yes, I know that! But do you? What will you do with her when you tire of this new game, Audrey? You can't just put her aside. You shall have to accept full responsibility for her until she's married—if she's married! She's a pretty little chit, but no beauty, and what about a settlement?"

Audrey waved a careless hand. "I shall, of course, make a settlement on her. With some nice clothes and a few parties, she'll have no trouble making a suitable match. London is crawling with all sorts of highly eligible men right now! The time couldn't be more perfect, with the peace celebrations! Why, she'll be engaged before the cat can lick her whisker, you wait and see!"

Miss Fishbank sighed. "I only hope you know what you're doing," she said.

"Of course I do!" Audrey sighed impatiently. "Don't I always?"

"No," Miss Fishbank replied frankly.

3

If Madam Celeste was surprised when one of her most sophisticated clients appeared in her atelier with a schoolroom miss in tow, she did not show it. This fashionable Frenchwoman was far too sophisticated to betray her emotions. As the most elegant modiste in London, she came forward herself to greet such a valued client. While Susan stared around herself, wide-eyed at the fashionable gowns displayed around the salon, Lady Wellford quickly spelled out her needs. "I'm bringing my niece out, Madam. Everything from underclothes to ball gowns are needed—right now."

Madam Celeste nodded understandingly. Behind her smile, she was already counting the many, many guineas Lady Wellford would be willing to spend. Her magic was not cheaply bought. Whatever she thought about the improbability of Lady Wellford sponsoring a debutante into the Polite World, that, fortunately, was not her problem. Turning this mouse into a sparkling creature was her only concern, and she studied Susan from all angles for several moments before snapping her fingers for an assistant.

"Take Miss into the dressing room and fit her with a proper corset," she commanded. "Everything new from the skin out!"

Before Susan could protest she was taken away, leaving Madam Celeste and Lady Wellford to ponder a wardrobe suitable for a debutante.

In due course, Susan was outfitted with a breathtaking number of morning dresses, afternoon dresses, dinner dresses, carriage cloaks, pelisses, and ball gowns. All of them were, of course, in the whites and pastels suitable to her status.

With Madam Celeste's promise that everything would be delivered to Half Moon Street within three days, Lady Wellford next directed her coachman to her milliner, where Susan was outfitted with hats, caps, and bonnets suitable to her new status, then onward, in the increasingly loaded barouche, to the mantua makers, for gloves, stockings, shawls, scarves, and other fripperies.

A last stop was made at Audrey's shoemaker, for shoes, sandals, boots, and dancing slippers. There must be many pairs of dancing slippers, Audrey commanded, for a female could wear out a single pair in an evening.

Susan, dazed and bedazzled by the largesse bestowed upon her could only repeat, again and again, her gratitude for such benevolence. "I feel as if I am in a fairy tale," she exclaimed as Audrey hustled her from one shop to the next. "There was never such a wonderful aunt as you!"

Audrey, as susceptible as the next person to flattery, merely smiled, enjoying the novel role of benefactor.

"I think we did very well, " she replied as Otterbine opened the door for them. "Tomorrow, we shall start to plan for your debut."

"Major Shelby is waiting in the Green Salon, my lady," the butler told her. "He has been here for quite some time."

Having temporarily forgotten all about the major, Audrey frowned. She found his calling at this moment quite inconvenient; she would have preferred to go upstairs with her niece and unwrap their new packages, some of which were hers. It would have been impossible for Audrey to shop without buying for herself.

"Run and find Miss Fishbank and ask her to help you sort out your things. Doubtless she will be greatly interested in your purchases," Audrey commanded her niece. "We will be dressing for dinner directly," she added, glancing at the hall clock. When she went shopping, it was so easy to lose track of time.

As she came into the Green Salon, Giles rose and crushed her into a passionate embrace. "My dearest Audrey—where have you been? I have been waiting for you forever!"

"You're crushing my hat, Giles," she said, quite unromantically. "You would not believe what has happened—"

But Giles was not to be so easily turned away from romance. He swept Audrey's hat into a chair and bent over her. "I want you now," he said huskily. "Waiting has been an agony!"

He was *so* handsome, Audrey thought as she allowed him to draw her towards him. How could she resist his ardor? Young and strong and handsome . . .

"Ahem!"

The sound of a masculine throat being cleared forced Giles and Audrey apart with the force of a wedge.

A man past his first youth slouched in the doorway, his hands thrust carelessly into his pockets. He was carelessly dressed in a loose-fitting coat and top boots, and a spotted kerchief that proclaimed him a member of the Four Horse Club. Deeply tanned and ruggedly featured, there was a slow, mocking grin spreading over his countenance. One eyebrow raised elequently, he shook his head.

"I fear I interrupt," he drawled.

"I *said*, sir," Otterbine puffed behind him, still holding his hat, "That I would *announce* you to her ladyship!" Behind him, Thomas and Charles, the footmen, loomed threateningly.

"And *I* said," the man replied without removing his mocking eyes from Audrey's, "that I would announce myself."

"You have a damned nerve, sir!" the major cried, thrusting out his chin. He moved toward the intruder, his fists clenched. Taking their cue from him, both the footmen moved in menacingly from behind.

Giles made an ugly sound in the back of his throat and lumbered toward him, raising his fists. Before the footmen could seize him, the man had planted a punch into the major's handsome jaw that sent him reeling backward. Giles fell into a chair, holding his cheek, momentarily stunned. "If either of you care for a taste of the same, come on, then," the man said coolly to the footmen, who drew back uncertainly.

Giles started up out of the chair, and before the man could move, had landed a blow into his midsection that sent him collapsing into Otterbine's arms. He puffed, and shook his head. "Well done!"

"Come on and get your cork drawn!" the major snarled, ready to offer it. One of the footmen whistled in admiration.

The stranger's smile deepened, and he raked Giles with a lazy look. "What do you box? Twelve stone? We must put on the gloves sometime, but right now, my business is with Lady Wellford." Audrey suddenly recognized him as the man she had seen in the park, and then at Carlton House. He had looked familiar then, and he looked familiar now.

"We can finish this right now! Have at, sirrah!" Giles lunged toward him just as the stranger straightened up and took a defensive stance. But Audrey stepped between them. "Stop it right now before you break something!" she exclaimed. "You, Giles, sit down and be quiet! And you, whoever you are—"

"Lord Merlin, at your service, ma'am," he said with an ironic bow.

"Are you both mad?" she demanded, striding across the room and staring up at him, her dark eyes flashing with rage. "How dare you storm into my house and start a fight? And you—" she turned, equally angry, toward Giles, and pointed a finger at him. "How dare you punch someone—*Lord Merlin?*"

He bowed again.

"Oh, hellfire and brimstone!" Audrey said involuntarily.

"Not quite all that bad, but—" he shrugged.

Nothing if not quick on her feet, Audrey peered at

him closely. "You're not Lord Merlin," she said. "Merlin is—"

"Sadly deceased. I am his heir, Nicholas Chance." the stranger replied. "The sixth Viscount Merlin, at your service, ma'am."

"Nicholas Chance . . .?" Audrey peered at him.

"Think back fifteen years, to a time when you were a schoolroom miss and I dunked your brother in the pond," he suggested.

"Oh . . ." Audrey said, and sat down. For the second time in twenty-four hours, she was nonplused.

"I say," Giles put in suspiciously, "You know this fella?"

Suddenly collecting that Otterbine and the footmen were still standing in the doorway watching all of this with vast and unprofessional interest, Audrey waved a weak hand in their direction. "Thank you, Otterbine. That will be all," she said repressively.

Otterbine, recalling himself, bowed and ushered the two footmen from the room, closing the doors firmly behind him. His professional demeanor firmly shaken, he shepherded his minions belowstairs, where he informed the housekeeper that this was not at all what he was used to in a gentleman's household, and mark his words, nothing good could come of the Young Lady's sudden descent upon them.

Happily impervious to the commotion in her domestic staff, Audrey confronted Lord Merlin—or, as she had known him, fifteen years ago, Nicholas Chance.

"She was a virago, even then," he was informing Major Shelby.

"Sir, you are speaking about a lady," Major Shelby said, rubbing his jaw. He was, Audrey noted for the first time, just a little pompous. How had she never seen that before?

"Virago? It was you who cut my braid off with your pocket knife!"

"Just so," Merlin replied. "I fear that my one childhood visit to my uncle's estate was unfortunate all the way around. My cousin, the *late* Lord Merlin, quarreled violently with my father. There was an estrangement. The result was that I came into the title somewhat unprepared—I have been living in India, you see." He smiled. "It was thought best that I be shipped away after I was sent down from Oxford. A young man's scandal! I think the family hoped that I would not return and my younger brother might succeed. His is a most respectable character, you see!"

"It would appear that time has not changed you in the least," Audrey said briskly. "What in the world possessed you to burst into my house in such a manner?"

"I was afraid you would deny me admittance otherwise," he replied calmly. Merlin thrust his hands deep into his pockets and leaned against the chimneypiece, very much at his ease. "I was given to believe by your brother that I would not be welcome in your home when you heard that I had come to see your niece."

"But she would be so happy to know that she need worry no longer, now that your uncle is dead! She won't have to marry him!"

Merlin raised one eyebrow. "There was never any question of my uncle marrying Miss Dysart! On the contrary, it is I who have been seeking her hand in marriage," he said. "You may imagine my feelings when I received an urgent message from your brother saying that Miss Dysart had run away from home. He thought she might seek shelter here with you. So, if you would be kind enough to tell her to fetch her things, I will take her home now."

"Certainly not! You cannot just burst in here and demand to remove my niece as if she were a stray animal! Susan said you were frightening, overbearing, and quite mad, and I see that she was not mistaken in her judgment," Audrey replied with spirit. "Do not think that I do not know what pressures were brought to bear on her by her father and That Woman, either, because I know them all too well! Even you would not expect a girl to marry where she cannot find regard, at the very least. But to force her to marry a man she fears—well!"

"Come now, I am not as black as I'm painted," Lord Merlin drawled. "At least let me speak with the girl. Her parents are quite worried about her."

"I don't think so," Audrey replied. "My niece has expressed a great dislike of you, and now that I have seen you for myself, I am inclined to agree with her. You were a thoroughly nasty boy, and you've become an odious man."

For a moment, Lord Merlin looked furious, his countenance dark as a thundercloud. Then, suddenly, he threw back his head and laughed. "Odious! By God, I've been called many names in my career, but never odious! Come now, my lady, send for your niece. I need to have her safely back to her parents before midnight. After all, she can't stay here, you know. That would never do!"

"Why not? I plan to bring her out and allow her to find a husband of her own choosing," Audrey said.

"*You?*" Lord Merlin asked. Up went the eyebrow again.

"What?" Giles demanded. "But—"

"Yes! I think she will make a perfectly lovely debutante!"

Lord Merlin laughed again. "You? Chaperone a debutante? Oh, Lord! That is a good joke! You're already nursemaiding this young whelp—"

"See here, sir!" Giles said, rising from his seat. "If you'd like another go-round—"

"I would, I would, but not here! Meet me tomorrow at Jackson's at eleven! Then you may have a chance at my liver and my lights! But if we have another go-round in the lady's salon, there's bound to be hell to pay!"

"There will be hell to pay anyway! If you two must engage in fisticuffs, better to do it where I don't have to see it! What makes you think that I cannot find my niece a husband? As far as I am able to see, marrying the dustman would be preferable to you! Susan has shown excellent sense!"

"Aunt Audrey, see—"

At that moment, Susan entered the room, accompanied by Miss Fishbank. She was wearing one of her new gowns, a pale jonquil crepe banded in silk lozenges, and her hair had been dressed high on her head. Her eye fell upon Lord Merlin and she uttered a little scream, taking a step backwards.

Fortunately, Giles was there to catch her, since she gave every indication of fainting dead away.

"You see?" Audrey turned to Nicholas. "The girl is terrified of you!"

"I will admit that I am odious," Lord Merlin said under his breath, "but I hardly think I am so terrible that the chit should faint dead away."

Susan shrank back from him, her eyes wide. She clutched at Giles's coat. "Please, do not make me go back to Bleakfriars," she pleaded. She was on the edge of hysteria.

"No one will make you go anywhere or do anything you do not want to do," Audrey promised her. "Isn't that right, Lord Merlin?"

"Exactly so. I had no idea that my presence so terrified you, Miss Dysart." He sounded faintly puzzled.

"Oh, I am so sorry, Lord Merlin! But I-I did not expect to see you here! I-I cannot marry you, Lord Merlin. Say I cannot, Aunt Audrey!" Susan shrank back against Major Shelby, who placed a protective hand on her shoulder.

For her part, Audrey wished the girl would show a little spirit. "No, no, of course not, " she answered.

Miss Fishbank had come forward now and placed a hand upon Susan's shoulder. "There, there, my dear," she said soothingly. "I'm sure there is nothing to fear." She peered at Lord Merlin closely. "Why," she said in tones of wonder, "It's Nicholas Chance, isn't it? Of course, you're Merlin now. My, how you've grown!"

"Is it Miss Fishbank?" Merlin asked, coming to shake her hand. "You at least, have not changed, ma'am! I find you just as I remember you."

"There, you see, my dear? I've known Lord Merlin since he was a boy! There's nothing to fear from him, I assure you!" Her tone was soothing, and after a moment, Susan was able to look up at him, if only just.

"I'm so embarrassed" she said at last. "Just *so*

embarrassed. But I can't marry you! I can't!"

"Please, do not start crying again, it is excessively tiresome," Audrey said. "No one is going to make you go home, or marry Lord Merlin, although I am a little vexed with you for allowing me to think that it was old Lord Merlin you meant, not this one!"

"But he *is* old!" Susan exclaimed.

"Out of the mouths of babes," Lord Merlin murmured. "I'm only thirty-eight!"

"*Ancient* to a girl of eighteen summers," Lady Wellford replied dryly. "Come now, Susan, do not be rude to poor Merlin! After all, he has stormed in here like young Lochinvar to rescue you."

"No need to be sarcastic," Giles said, somewhat more sharply than was his wont in addressing Audrey. "Miss Dysart! I will admit that I had my reservations about your presence in your aunt's household. I see now that they were motivated purely by jealousy, that the time she spent with you would be time taken away from me. But I can now see that your circumstances are such that any *true* gentleman can—indeed *must* lend his support to you!" He glared up at Merlin as he spoke.

His lordship whistled. "Very prettily spoken! Oh, no need to glare at me in such a way, Major—you see, I know who you are! The famous Major Shelby, hero of Spain! You'll have your turn to pummel me tomorrow at Jackson's Boxing Saloon! Miss Fishbank, your servant! Audrey, until later. . . ."

With that, Lord Merlin took his leave.

"You are *that* Major Shelby?" Susan asked, completely distracted from her present trials by this piece of news.

The major looked pleased, but merely blushed. "I

had the honor to be mentioned in a few dispatches—"

Audrey was incapable of allowing Merlin to leave without having the last word. Picking up her skirts, she followed him into the hall, where he was retrieving his hat. "Odious doesn't begin to describe you, Nicholas! You were an obnoxious child, and you've become an obnoxious, rude, overbearing man, and I wouldn't let my niece marry you if you were the last man left in England!"

Merlin paused before the gilt mirror in the hallway and carefully adjusted his high-crowned beaver hat over his nut-brown locks. He turned, took his walking stick from the chair, and put his hand on the doorknob. From blue eyes, he gave Audrey a long, level look. "No need to worry. I'll show myself out." He smiled, and his mocking expression infuriated her more than mere words could have done. "I shall thoroughly enjoy the spectacle of the, ah, *reknowned and sophisticated* Lady Wellford bringing out a debutante! And I shall enjoy seeing precisely what manner of man you select for her husband! Perhaps one of the Regent's cronies? An actor? Or one of your so-called *intellectual* friends? Your reputation precedes you wherever you go, Audrey."

Before her indignation could find words, he had closed the door behind him.

Audrey picked up a vase from the hall table and seriously considered running into the street and pitching it at Merlin's head.

Under other circumstances, she might have done so, for she was completely used to following her impulses. However, with a deep, shuddering breath, she managed to check her temper, reminding herself that such a gesture would simply prove Merlin's point. It would prove that she was not capable of chaperoning Susan, let alone finding her a suitable match. Audrey lowered the vase. She took another deep breath, looked at her reflection in the mirror and went back into the Green Salon with as much dignity as she could muster.

"Oh, there you are!" Giles greeted her with a satisfied smile. "Audrey, I have had the most wonderful idea! My mother and m'sisters are in London for the Season. They have taken a house in Upper Mount Street. Tomorrow, you and Miss Dysart will call on them, and you and Mama may put your heads together about bringing my sisters and Miss Dysart out together! This way, you will have a chance to meet my family, so that when you do say you will marry me, Mama will be a little more equitable to the idea!"

"Is the major not the most brilliant man you have ever met in your life?" Susan breathed happily, gazing at him adoringly.

"Oh yes, brilliant," Audrey said. "My cup runneth over." She forced herself to smile.

4

"More tea, Lady Wellford?"

"No, thank you, this is fine."

"I can't understand what is keeping Giles. He said he would be back by one. Perhaps you would care for a glass of sherry?"

"That would be—that is, no thank you."

"Lady Wellford never drinks spirits before dinner," said Miss Fishbank primly.

No good deed, it is said, goes unpunished. And Lady Wellford was beginning to feel very punished indeed as she balanced a teacup and a macaroon in her hands and forced her smile to stay firmly in place. It may have looked like a ghastly mask to Appie, but the former governess's composure remained unruffled as she held out her own cup for a drop more Earl Grey.

Becoming respectable, Audrey thought as she sipped

her tea and listened to Major Shelby's mother talk about her children, was deadly dull. And for a restless spirit like Audrey's, boredom was never far from the surface.

And the fact that Giles was nowhere to be seen added to her annoyance. Without his presence, this visit was somewhat strained as both sides grappled for conversational topics.

Not, she reminded herself sternly, that Charlotte Shelby was stuffy or unkind. A quiet Devonshire widow left to raise three children on her own, she was miles away in character and interest from the dashing Lady Wellford. Her daughters, Emily and Jane, were lively, well-brought-up young ladies with whom Susan had formed an instant bond, and it was clear that mother and daughters all adored their heroic Giles unquestioningly—so much so that it never occurred to any of them to question his eagerness to foster a friendship between them and the dashing Lady Wellford and her pretty niece, it seemed to Audrey.

Although she had taken great pains to pull together a matronly ensemble, in subdued shades of blue, with long sleeves, a high neck, and only her pearls for ornament, she still felt entirely too dashing in contrast to Mrs. Shelby in her simple yet elegant dove-gray merino morning dress, with a pretty cap tied over her fading gold hair.

There was a noise in the hallway, and Mrs. Shelby turned, a little relief on her face. "That must be Giles. Now we shall find out what made him so late."

But when Giles came into the room, sporting a purple, half-swollen eye and a look of sheepish triumph, his mother and sisters exclaimed in horror.

It was nothing, however, to Audrey's dismay when

she saw that he was accompanied by Lord Merlin, whose jaw was decidedly swollen.

"Sorry I'm late," Giles said, ready to be defensive, "but you wouldn't have believed what a bang-up morning Merlin and I have had—oh, Mama, may I present Lord Merlin, Merlin, m'mother and those two flibbertigibbets in the corner are m'sisters, Emily and Jane! Audrey, Miss Fishbank, I do apologize, but you do understand how it was!"

Merlin bowed over Mrs. Shelby's hand. "I came along to ensure that you had my apologies in person, ma'am! I realize that boxing is considered by most ladies to be an intolerable sport, but your son is no mean talent in the ring! Gave me as good as he gave at Spain! Even the great Jackson himself was impressed."

Instead of being horrified, Mrs. Shelby seemed merely amused. "Men! What is one to do with them?" she asked her guests.

Audrey, who could think of several possibilities, bit her lower lip and continued to smile as Lord Merlin bent over her hand. "Ah, my dear old friend Audrey, how very nice to see you here! An unexpected pleasure."

"I say, Audrey, I know it's bad of me, but you should see Merlin strip! He's a bruising fighter and a downy one!" Giles exclaimed. "What a left hook!"

Audrey gave them both a baleful look. Men, she understood better than anyone, were quick to shift their alliances when matters of sport, hunting, and politics were involved. Nonetheless, she had expected better.

"Men will go on their starts, no matter what. Giles, you are very bad, however, to leave these ladies waiting for you so long, and you owe them all an apology. If they do not accept it, that is your misfortune, for you were very bad to forget them." Try as she might, it was obvious that Mrs. Shelby had great difficulty being angry with her son.

His sisters, however were quick to rally him on his poor manners, and Giles spiritedly defended himself. Audrey noted that Merlin greeted Susan with the same offhanded civility he paid to Giles's sisters, and that she did not shrink so much from his presence today. Perhaps finding friends of her own age had given her more confidence.

"We are always glad to have Giles's friends," Mrs. Shelby said, gesturing Merlin toward a seat. "Will you take a cup of tea? Or a glass of sherry?"

"Sherry would be just the thing. Are these macaroons? Delicious! Thank you so much, Mrs. Shelby."

To Audrey's great amazement, Lord Merlin exerted himself to be charming to his hostess and succeeded admirably. He complimented her on her son's heroism and her daughters' manners and discovered a mutual acquaintance in India. With a self-deprecating humor, he recounted some of his Indian adventures and promised that at some not too distant point, he would invite them all to his house on Pall Mall to see some of the examples of Indian arts and crafts he had gathered in his journeys around the subcontinent. With the young people occupied around the piano-forte, the conversation turned toward earlier days.

"I recall my own Season very well," Mrs. Shelby was saying. "It was the summer of eighty-nine. When did you come out, Lady Wellford?"

"Oh, much later than that," Audrey said vaguely.

"It was the Little Season of ninety-seven," Lord Merlin said. "I recall it well."

"I was very young to come out, everyone said so," Audrey said quickly. If looks could kill, Merlin would have been dead on the floor. Happily, Giles was turning the pages as Susan played a country tune, and missed that interesting piece of information.

This Season, Mrs. Shelby told Lord Merlin, was the first time she had been in the Metropolis for many years. She had hopes of launching her daughters successfully, and she was grateful for Lady Wellford's kindness to her son. "For you may depend upon it, a young man in the city needs the counsel of older friends who may guide him in the right direction," she said earnestly. "It would be easy for his head to be turned by those attracted to his new fame."

"Indeed," Merlin replied, straight-faced. "I am certain that Lady Wellford has been an excellent mentor. No one, I am convinced, takes more of an interest in the welfare of young people."

"Oh, I am sure that you could show me a thing or two," Audrey said with a smile.

Merlin bowed in her direction. "I am completely at your service, Audrey, as you know. Any small service I may render you, you have but to ask."

"Why, Merlin, how extremely generous of you!" Audrey crowed. "You know, Mrs. Shelby, Merlin House has one of the finest ballrooms in London! You remember it, don't you, Appie, from the old lord, when he was still entertaining? Quite grand—why, I believe it can hold five hundred people! It would be a perfect place to launch the girls. And if we were to bring them all out together, we could have quite a squeeze! All London would be there!"

For once, Merlin looked discomfited. "But that room has not been opened up in years! It's all in dustcovers and it would need painting and—" His eyes met Audrey's and he shrugged. "It can be made ready as soon as possible. You only have to pick a date," he finished.

Mrs. Shelby was suitably grateful. If she had noted Lady Wellford twisting Lord Merlin's arm, she was far too practical to make any comment. She was wise enough to understand that presenting her daughters beneath the aegis of a rich and fashionable woman such as Lady Wellford would elevate them far beyond what she could expect to accomplish on her own. If Lady Wellford could convince her son's friend to allow them to use Merlin House, it would be a great thing.

"We shall put our heads together and come up with a suitable date, Merlin," Audrey promised. "And you need not bother your head about the rest of it. Appie is a marvel at organizing parties! She always knows how to get the right champagne, and where one may find extra footmen and all of that sort of thing! I could never entertain without her."

Miss Fishbank inclined her head. "You may leave all the details to us," she said gravely.

Thus routed, Lord Merlin soon took his leave, promising to call again.

The ladies, left to their own devices, put their heads together. "I would be glad of your guidance, to be completely honest," Audrey told Mrs. Shelby. "I know very little about managing a debut."

If Mrs. Shelby had deduced this information on her own, she was too kind to say so. Instead, she smiled. "Then perhaps between the two of us, we may accomplish it, for having lived so long in the country,

I am sadly out of touch with the Polite World, and I would like to see my daughters acquire a little town bronze. You, Lady Wellford, would know what plays are to be seen, what events they should attend in the peace celebrations far better than I."

Audrey assured her that she knew exactly what was fashionable, and could procure tickets for all the right plays and entertainments. She was happy to recommend Madam Celeste for gowns and Hookham's Lending Library for the latest books, and to promise that her coachman should take Mrs. Shelby and the girls up in the park at the fashionable hour.

"As to theater tickets, my dear friend Emma Hart can no doubt be use to us there, for she, of course—" Audrey promised, then faltered. She began to foresee stormy waters ahead.

"You know Emma Hart?" Mrs. Shelby asked.

"She is a very good friend of mine," Audrey said firmly.

"Oh, I remember her so well in *Romeo and Juliet,* many years ago, when my husband was still alive. She quite moved me to tears. Is she still on the stage? I should love to have my girls see her in a play."

Audrey almost sighed with relief. "She's playing *Mary of Scotland* at Drury Lane. I have a box there. I would be happy to take the girls to see her play."

"I'm sure they would love it above all things," Mrs Shelby said.

"I see you two are finding things to talk about," Giles said, coming over and putting his hand on Audrey's shoulder.

"Oh, yes!" Mrs. Shelby said, gazing fondly at her son. "We are quite a pair of parents, worrying about the next generation."

* * *

"Vouchers for Almack's?" Lady Jersey asked. Her silvery laugh pealed out. "For *Audrey?* Nicholas, have you run mad?"

"Only for you, Sally," Merlin said. He looped his arm through that of the lady and steered her through the Royal Academy's exhibit. "The thing of it is, she's going to ask you, and it is going to pain her sorely to do so, but she has a niece she's attempting to launch on the ton. Quite unexceptionable, a Miss Dysart."

"Not, I pray, a daughter of Bob Dysart's! Poor thing!"

"Not poor at all. She's rather a taking little thing."

Lady Jersey cast him a shrewd look. "Thinking of settling down at last, Nick?"

He raised an eyebrow and shook his head. "Not me, Sally, you know me better than that. "

"I thought perhaps some exotic Indian beauty would have captured you by now." Lady Jersey fanned herself.

"Oh, no, I am impervious to romance. You know that I have no heart. Here's a Turner for you. Look at the painter's work on that sky over Southwark. Brilliant."

"Yes, quite beautiful. But why are you being so excessively interested in Audrey Wellford and her niece?"

"Oh, I have my reasons. The thing of it is, Sally, will you do this for me?"

"Will she have the Adonis in tow? Lord, what a handsome young man. He quite takes one's breath away." Lady Jersey nodded to an acquaintance across the gallery and peered into her programme. "*Portrait of a Lady* by Hayter, and that is no lady, that's Pitt's mistress, that Palmer female. She looks like the cat that ate the canary, too."

"Astute observer that you are! I will also need vouchers for the Adonis's mother and sisters. The widow is in from the country, trying to see her daughters creditably settled. Now, before you say you cannot have every rustic squire's widow within your hallowed halls, think about this; the Adonis's mother and sisters guarantee you the Adonis. Major Shelby is quite the social catch this Season. That should give his mother and sisters a certain cachet. Good West Country family, no need to blush for their manners."

Lady Jersey sighed. "I suppose you would also like me to have a ball for these people. Why not just ask me for the moon, Nick?"

"I knew I could count on you!" Merlin said. "And remember, Sally, not a word to anyone!"

"Very well! I am putty in your hands! I only wish that I knew what you are about, Nicholas!"

He brought her hand to his lips. "When I find that out, you will be the first to know!" he promised.

5

"*Respectable?*" *Emma Hart's* generous mouth curved upward in a smile and she reached for another sweetmeat. Ensconced on the chaise in Audrey's boudoir, she settled in for a comfortable chat. "My dear Audrey, I have played many roles on the stage, but *respectable* is not among them. Unless of course, you count the time I played the mother of the Gracchi in *The Roman Secret.*"

"I can hardly go about in a toga all day," Audrey replied, her head buried deep in her enormous wardrobe. "What do you think about this?" She held up a wine-colored dinner dress of *gros de naples* trimmed in black jet beads.

"Too décolleté!" Madam Hart pronounced. "You could wear that black pellerine over it so you don't show so much bosom. Where is your niece, anyway?"

"Out with Giles's mother and sisters to see the victory parade through the park. I pled a headache for that event, you may be sure. Giles's mother is a godsend. She *enjoys* taking Susan with her. And very, very respectable. You should have read the letter I sent to Robert and That Woman. It will singe the hairs on her chin. What about this?" She held up an emerald and silver striped ball gown, deeply hemmed with a band of silver lace.

"Dashing. Very dashing. If you wore a turban with it, however, you might look respectable."

"A turban?" Audrey looked horrified. "Must I wear a *turban?*"

"Turbans," Emma Hart pronounced, "*Very* respectable. Only the highest sticklers wear them."

"And old ladies with five chins who live in Bath."

"Sarah Siddons and Mrs. Fitzherbert both wear turbans," Emma pointed out reasonably.

"And look what happened to them," Audrey replied. "No turbans!" She opened a box and pulled out a sweeping blue silk bonnet, trimmed with enormous ruches and rosettes of ribbon. Placing it on her head, she turned to look at her friend. Madam Hart squinted at it and popped another sweet in her mouth.

"Fashionable, but respectable. Not that little velvet evening toque with the diamond clip, though—too dashing by half!"

"But that was what I was going to wear tonight! It looks very well with my azure satin, just tilted a little over my ear."

"Fashionable, yes, but not—respectable. Respectable is just a little past the fashion, high to the neck, long in the sleeve, just a hue subdued; respectable is—"

"Respectable is deadly dull," Audrey said, throwing the bonnet across the room. It landed in a large pile of discarded dresses thrown carelessly across a couch. "You are so lucky not to be respectable," she added sulkily.

Madam received this comment in the spirit in which it was given. She stretched out her hand, examined her new turquoise and diamond ring, a gift from Sir Peyton, and peeled a chocolate rusk. "But I did not agree to bring out my niece, either. I have two nieces. One is married to a greengrocer in Whitechapel and the other is married to a public house keeper in Notting Hill Gate."

"For the past week, I have done nothing but show Susan and the Shelbys the Metropolis. We have been to Astley's Amphitheater, the Marine Parade, Hookham's Library, the Royal Academy show, to the Elgin Marbles, the Wellington fireworks, Somerset House, and I do not know how many breakfasts, teas, and parties. I have drunk enough tea to float a battleship. I have smiled and smiled and made inane conversation until I thought my head would fall off. I sit along the wall with the other old tabbies and watch a group of very young people dance. Why, I dare not dance more than two dances with Giles, lest we cause a whisper of scandal. As for finding any time *alone* with him, I dare not!"

"What a shame," Emma sighed. "And things were going along so well before all of this happened."

"Well, at least he's not pressing me to marry him."

"Marriage was not what I had in mind, my dear," Madam Hart laughed. She turned. "Now, tell me about Lord Merlin."

Before Audrey could reply, Wescott bustled into

the room. She tsked at the pile of discarded clothing and immediately began to set it to rights with a great deal of clucking and shaking of her head.

"I wish you would talk some sense into my lady, Madam Hart," she said. "A whole season's lovely new wardrobe she has, and she wants to stuff her bodice with lace and hide her lovely hair under caps!"

"There is a price to be paid for being respectable," Madam Hart replied philosophically.

Wescott sniffed. "We never had this sort of nonsense before the Young Lady came here," she muttered under her breath.

"My, look at the time," Emma drawled. She picked up the last rusk off the plate, "Why, I must be getting to the theater or I shall be late." The rusk disappeared. With a swirl of shawls and cloaks, she arose from the chaise. "Never mind, darling, I shall see myself out."

In an aside to Wescott she hissed, "Patience! Patience! You know how easily she bores!"

"I heard that!" Audrey cried. "Out! Out! And don't think I don't know that you've been trying to lure Wescott away from me for years, because I do!"

"The very idea!" both actress and abigail said at once in such affronted tones that Audrey knew it was true. Since she also knew Wescott would never stoop to work for an actress for half the wages she paid, she was able to shrug it off.

Madam Hart turned at the door. "See you at the theater tonight. If you want to bring your party to my dressing room during the entr'acte, I promise that I shall send all the rakes and coxcombs away! It will be quite—respectable!"

With this Parthian shot, she made her exit in a

cloud of shawls and scent. It was a departure worthy of a great actress.

"Look at this!" Wescott almost wailed, picking up the discarded *gros de naples*. "Now I shall have to take this downstairs and iron it all over again if you are to wear it tonight!"

The abigail bustled off, shaking her head, bearing away the offending gown.

Alone at last, Audrey threw herself down on the chaise abandoned by Emma and sighed, putting her feet up and closing her eyes. If she could just rest for a moment in peace and quiet, she thought—

And then, something collapsed on top of her.

"*Mph!*" Audrey said, but her words were smothered as a pair of moist lips crushed themselves against hers. "Giles!"

Giles raised himself from the chaise. "I thought I should never get you alone, my dearest! Now, before anything else happens, let us—"

"How in the world did you get in? I thought you were taking the girls to the victory parade!"

"I did, and now we are back! Without you, it was a dead bore! As soon as the field was clear, I hied up the back stairs to your bedroom—almost reconnoitered with your woman coming down! Had to lurch back into an alcove to hide. But here I am, my beloved! It seems like forever since we were alone! Let us seize the moment while we have it—"

Sorely tempted though she was, Audrey sighed and disengaged Giles's muscular arms from her person. "Where are the girls?" she asked.

"In Susan's room, doing whatever it is females do," Giles said carelessly. "What does it matter? Kiss me, my beautiful Audrey—"

"What would your mother say?" Audrey demanded. "What if your sisters and my niece should happen to walk in? A nice thing that would be—"

"You never cared about such things before," Giles sighed. "I suppose you're right. But only say you'll marry me, Audrey, and—"

"Oh, Giles, hellfire and brimstone! Giles, you are handsome, brave, and impetuous—and impossible." Audrey gave him a litte peck and gently disengaged herself from his embrace. "Giles." A terrible thought had risen to her mind. "You have not actually *said* anything to your mother or your sisters about us, have you?"

The major had the grace to blush. "No. I thought it would be better if she had a chance to get to know you before I announced my intentions."'

"Good," Audrey sighed, much relieved. "Giles, you must understand my position has changed. My conduct must be extremely circumspect if I am to be able to sponsor Susan. There must be no reason for anyone to suspect that you and I are anything more than good friends."

The major's handsome face turned sulky. "Hang what other people think—"

"Giles, can you honestly tell me that your mother would be delighted to know that you have developed a liaison with a widow slightly older than yourself?"

"Well, I don't think she'll be overjoyed, but when she gets to know you as I do, she will love you too! I thought perhaps this might be a chance for her to come to know what a *good* person you are, in spite of that fact you and m'mother are as alike as chalk and cheese. Although, truth to tell, I don't much enjoy this new side of you. There are times I wish that chit had never appeared on your doorstep! Audrey, I thought that you and I would see more of each other. Instead it seems like we spend less time together now than we did before And I want you, Audrey. You don't know what it's like to burn for you the way I do."

"Indeed I do understand. But there can be no breath of scandal, Giles, not while I am responsible for an innocent girl. I have undertaken the responsibility of looking after her, and there can be no turning back now."

"You don't care about me anymore," Giles sighed. His golden profile, caught in the afternoon light, shone like the head on a Greek coin. His fair curls, his military mustache, his long lashes, the strong lines of his jaw, the solid muscle that heaved with every breath beneath his scarlet hussar uniform, his well-turned thighs in their tight buckskin breeches, the male scent of him, like sunlight and clean linen, were enough to melt a stoic far harder than Audrey.

"Giles, you know that's not true!" she exclaimed.

"Then let me, let us have this one moment," he cried, pressing his advantage, sweeping her into his arms and holding her until she thought she would swoon. His lips pressed against hers, seeking assuagement and union. She could feel his passion and wanted, with all of her being, to return it.

Somehow, she found the discipline to gently draw herself away from him. Only a fool or a nun could not regret those shoulders, that longing. What woman does not dream of a knight-errant, a young and virile man, handsome as a Greek god, a man whose passions are devoted solely to her? Certainly not Audrey, who was powerless to resist the charms of her lusty solider.

Save for the tiny bat-squeak of a voice in the back of her mind that whispered, *This isn't what you want, my girl.*

It was simply that at that moment, it was awfully hard to hear that little voice over the rush of blood from her beating heart.

Just as Audrey was about to surrender, there was a knock at the door.

"Aunt? It's Susan! May I come in?"

"Damn." Giles sighed, rolling away on his back and looking up at the ceiling.

"Quick!' Audrey hissed. "Out of here!"

"My lady, do what I might, these creases will not come out!" Wescott's voice drifted up the back staircase.

Under less trying circumstances, the expression on Giles's face might have been amusing. He looked about himself wildly, while Audrey sat up and rearranged the sash on her dressing gown.

"Not in the wardrobe! That's the first place she'll look!" Audrey whispered.

"Aunt Audrey, are you awake?"

Giles, soldier that he was, thought on his feet. He strode across the room and threw open a window, silently folding his muscular frame through the frame. "Farewell, my lovely one," he whispered.

While Audrey watched, horrified, he disappeared from sight.

The curtains billowed out in the wind as Wescott bustled into the room. "Say what you will about *gros de naples,* it wrinkles sadly, and getting it to stay straight takes steam, which I do not have time to do tonight. I suggest you wear the nile green with the silver net overskirt, my lady. The color flatters you, and—" She looked suspiciously at the open window.

"I thought it was a trifle close in here," Audrey said, quickly moving toward the curtains. She looked down in time to see a flash of scarlet uniform in the boxwood garden, heading toward the mews. At the same time, she saw Miss Fishbank clipping roses in the arbor.

"Aunt Audrey?"

"Please do come in!" Audrey called, patting her hair into place. It looked awfully like Miss Fishbank had seen that flash of scarlet uniform, too. "Hellfire and brimstone," Audrey muttered under her breath.

Before she had time to discern anything more, Susan had admitted herself into the room. She was every inch the young lady of fashion, attired in a walking dress of jaconet weave with a smart buff spencer trimmed with epaulets and frogs. Over her dark curls she wore a little toque, trimmed in gold braid in the military style. Her eyes were shining, and there were two spots of rose in her cheeks. The transformation from the wilted schoolroom miss she had been only ten days ago was astonishing, and Audrey had no compunctions in feeling a wave of self-congratulation on the change. "Aunt Audrey!" Susan exclaimed. "I wish you could have come! It was the most wonderful thing! We saw General Blücher and all the generals, and the Tsar, and the Prince Regent and the Royal Dukes, and Lord Wellington, I mean, *the Duke* of Wellington! He was so gracious as to bow to our carriage as he rode past! He is a frosty-looking man, is he not? I would be quite terrified of him, Major Shelby says he's a military genius. Major Shelby bought us all little Union Jack flags from a stallkeeper, and we waved them as he went past! You should have heard the crowd! There was such a *roar* for the Duke and the Tsar!"

"Indeed! I'm so sorry I missed it," Audrey said mendaciously. She was glad, however, that Susan was enjoying herself. Lord knew, little enough had happened to the girl until she had come to London.

"But when the Regent and his brothers rode by, everyone booed and hissed," Susan added. "I had no idea that he was so unpopular! And they were something of a disappointment, all of them like so many overfed toads, fat and quite old!"

Audrey gave a gurgle of laughter. "They don't think of themselves as fat and old, not a bit of it," she informed her wide-eyed niece. "You might not know it now, to look at him, but there was a time when the Regent was considered the handsomest man in Europe."

Susan looked very doubtful indeed. "He looks like a shocking loose screw," she said firmly.

"Susan Dysart! Where did you learn such a shocking expression?" Audrey demanded.

"Why, from you, Aunt Audrey," Susan replied ingenuously. "Don't you remember, that's what you said about—"

"Never mind," Audrey sighed. She gestured to Susan to sit down beside her. Facing her niece, she studied her earnest, eager face. The girl would never be a great beauty, she decided, but a new hairstyle, a change of wardrobe, and a little excitement had certainly enhanced her looks considerably. There was certainly no fault with her looks, which were fresh and pleasant. The Dysarts, whatever their other faults, were a handsome clan. Her figure was slim and graceful. Released from the burden of a repressive regime, she was lively and enthusiastic, and her manners were engaging. True, Susan's understanding was hardly profound, something that taxed Audrey's patience, never her strong suit. But then, in Audrey's experience, most men liked a woman whose intelligence was not a challenge to their own. If you added the few thousand pounds a year that she would settle on her niece, she was an eligible young lady indeed. Being seen in public with Mrs. Shelby and her daughters would provide eligible gentlemen with a chance to see and wonder who she was. By the time she was presented, they would be anxious to meet her.

Oblivious to her aunt's thoughts, Susan was gazing at Audrey with enormous, adoring eyes, rather like a puppy. It was not an attitude that made Audrey comfortable. She knew herself well enough to know that she was no one for a young girl to emulate.

"Susan." she said carefully, "Sometimes I may say things that are not suitable for you to repeat. There is a great deal of fashionable cant that is shockingly blue, and you ought to be careful what you repeat."

Susan's response was to look very dejected indeed. Two tears welled up in her blue eyes. "Oh, Aunt, I am so sorry," she exclaimed. "I don't mean to do anything that would upset you." She blinked. "It's just that I would like to be just like you. So beautiful, and so fashionable. I would give anything to have a handsome man like the major in love with me."

"Please, don't cry, my dear! I meant no harm. It is just that you are still learning how to go about. You see, I am a widow, and Society allows me certain rules of conduct that would not be seen as suitable for you."

"Are you going to send me home?" Susan asked, her lower lip quivering.

"Of course not! Don't be such a goose! Dry your eyes. Tonight, we are going to the theater with Mrs. Shelby and her daughters, and I know you will like that! We will see Madam Hart play Mary of Scotland, and she has asked me to invite you all back stage during the entr'acte. So you must look pretty, and not as if you had been weeping, or Madam will think you didn't like her performance, which would hurt her feelings dreadfully. And a wounded Madam, believe me, is a terror!"

This rallied Susan somewhat, and she forced a little smile.

"That's better," Audrey said gently. "Now, my dear, there's something else we need to talk about. You will be meeting a great many gentlemen soon, if you have not met a few already, and you will doubtless find that you have admirers. Beaux."

Susan nodded a little uncertainly. The idea of beaux quite naturally caught her attention, and she folded her hands in her lap and looked expectantly at her aunt.

"Sooner or later, one of them may engage your affection. If things go the way they should, he will be the right gentleman for you. However, there are many *wrong* gentlemen out there, too. And these are the ones you want to avoid." Audrey held up her fingers and ticked them off. "Married men, half-pay officers, gazetted fortune hunters, inveterate gamblers, hardened flirts, lascivious rakes, dandies, counter-coxcombs, Corinthians, peep o' day boys, coxcombs, *anyone* in the Prince Regent's set, and poets. Poets are particularly fatal! Why, I remember one who—" Audrey looked down at her fingers. "That seems like almost every man in Society!" she sighed. "But, my dear, if nothing else, you can learn from my experience. Have you met anyone so far who interests you, my dear? We can make sure that he receives an invitation to the ball."

Susan flushed up to the roots of her hair and looked away. "No, no, there is no one," she replied quickly. It looked for a moment like she was going to cry again, and Audrey felt a stab of impatience. Obviously, there was no one yet, and the chit felt bad about it. "There, there, my dear, there's a whole Season ahead of you! Balls and parties and entertainments, and I am sure I will be able to get vouchers for Almack's, too. You will meet many, many gentlemen, I promise you. And one will be your Prince Charming! But he should also be suitable. We should know his family, he should have a comfortable income, be a member of the Church of England, and of course, have no bad habits or questionable associations. Believe me, I have put a great deal of thought into this, Susan. And I think that you are a good, sensible girl who will allow me to give you a hint about how you ought to go on."

Susan nodded a little dispiritedly.

Audrey had an awful thought. "You haven't met someone, have you? Someone who's not quite the thing?"

For a moment, an odd look crossed the girl's face, but it was gone before Audrey fully comprehended that shoals might lie ahead. "I am very grateful to you, Aunt Audrey, and I will try to do what you think is best," she said in a little voice.

If only Susan would show a little fire, some flash, she might become more interesting, Audrey thought. *If only,* Audrey thought, *she would show a little more* bottom. It had taken considerable courage to run away from home, to board a public stagecoach and find her way to a strange house in a strange city. But now that she was here, she seemed to have lost that spirit. If a man ignited that—well!

She patted Susan's hand. "Now, go and change for dinner. We'll be leaving for the theater right afterwards. I'm so glad we had this little talk," she said. "It helps us to understand each other better, don't you think?"

"Oh, yes," Susan breathed. She paused. "There is only one other thing that I think—"

"What's that? I am here to help you in whatever way I can."

Susan twisted her hands in her lap. "Mama said that when I married Lord Merlin she would explain to me—that is—well, what married people do together! Can you tell me, Aunt Audrey?"

It was Audrey's turn to flush.

"Go ask Miss Fishbank," she said brightly. "She is very good at explaining things."

Truly, this was turning out to be just a little more difficult than Lady Wellford had expected.

A solution to at least one of her problems, however, came that very evening at Drury Lane. Like many solutions, it took an unexpected form.

Mrs. Shelby and Lady Wellford took the foremost chairs, surveying the audience and the other boxes in search of acquaintances and celebrities. Seeing some activity in the royal box, they fell to speculating about the Tsar, whose sister the Grand Duchess Catherine had recently joined him in the Metropolis and had promptly set tongues wagging with her arrogant behavior.

"I think I can say this box holds the loveliest women at Drury Lane tonight," Giles said as he seated his mother in Lady Wellford's box.

"And the best-looking man." Susan sat as he held her chair for her. She flushed slightly and dropped her eyes to the fan in her lap, biting her lower lip.

Giles, seating himself between her and his sisters, smiled. "You flatter me, Miss Dysart. But I must say you are looking very becomingly tonight."

Susan glanced up at him from beneath her lashes. "Do you think so? I-I am glad to hear it. That, that is—you are so knowledgeable and wise in the ways of the world that—that one must needs always heed your opinion!" Why, she thought, did she always feel so tongue-tied whenever she tried to talk to the major? Alone, she could imagine a thousand witty things she might say to him. But when they were together, she felt as if her mind were made of cotton and her legs of blancmange. He was so wise, so handsome, such a hero!

"Well, I may not be slap up to the mark in all things, but I thank you for thinking so!" Giles replied. "In truth, Miss Dysart, I have noticed in the past few days that you are looking very becomingly."

"My aunt is to be thanked for that," Susan admitted. "She has such wonderful style, and is so fashionable herself. I am so grateful to her for all her kindness to me! Since you were there when I came, I need not elaborate!"

"Oh, yes, Audrey is a knowing 'un!" Giles murmured absently. He cleared his throat. "She is everything that is admirable." But it was Susan he was looking at when he said this. And she was in her best looks, wearing a pink-and-white striped gown, her hair dressed high on her head, a string of pearls clasped around her neck, small diamond-and-pearl drops in her ears, gifts from Audrey, who declared no lady could be without a set of those most precious jewels. "The diamonds and emeralds can come later," she had said. "But pearls a lady must have always."

Having never been to the theater before, Susan looked at everything about her with wide eyes and a great interest, from the stage, where the curtain had not yet risen, to the pit, where apprentices and other City workers were preparing to cheer their favorites and jeer those who had fallen beneath their disapproval. Giles answered all her questions, which were many, and called her attention to the presence of visiting Royalty. There were many celebrated Allied commanders in town for the celebrations, and he took pleasure in pointing them all out to her, basking in her admiration of his knowledge and expertise.

Several people dropped past the box, as much to discover the identity of the four unknown but very striking ladies as to pay their respects to a reigning queen of fashionable London. That several of them were eligible men pleased Audrey very much.

Audrey made introductions and was gratified to be promised a number of invitations to forthcoming parties, routs, and balls. In turn she promised several people invitations to their ball at Merlin House.

She was in such an elevated mood that she was even able to smile at Lord Merlin when he slunk lazily into the doorway.

"This box is a veritable flower garden of lovely

females," he drawled, bowing over Mrs. Shelby's hand and greeting the major and the girls with careless civility. It was to Lady Wellford that he directed his attention, his gaze sweeping over her ensemble with a practiced eye. "Ah, Audrey, you are in fine form tonight," he said with a mocking smile. "Very fetching fichu. Planning to set a new fashion?"

Aware that he was poking fun at the expanse of lace she had used to fill in the low neckline of her gown, she frowned. A biting retort rose to her lips, but she suppressed it in favor of what she hoped was a withering smile. "And *you* look so well turned out! Have you hired a valet?"

Merlin cast a careless glance at his black evening clothes, accented by a snowy cravat, tied *à l'anglaise*. "I have even worn knee britches for this evening! Am I not a perfect model of a dandy?" he asked regretfully. "I clean up fairly well, you know, when I have a mind to do so."

"Sally," Audrey said quickly, looking over his shoulder at a new guest. "How good to see you! Lady Jersey, may I present my guests to you?"

Lady Jersey, all fluttering and laughter, was inclined to be gracious. She was introduced to each guest in turn, and after gushing only a little over the handsome major, said, "You must allow me to send you all vouchers for Almack's! Audrey, it is a great deal too bad of you not to let me know you were bringing out your niece, or I would have done so earlier!"

Trying to conceal her surprise, Audrey said everything that was proper and promised that her dear friend Sally should receive invitations to the forthcoming ball.

"Lord Merlin has been kind enough to offer us the

use of the ballroom at Merlin House," Mrs. Shelby said.

Lady Jersey absorbed this information with only the smallest upturn of her lips. A light appeared in her eye, however.

At that moment, the house lights were dimmed, and after exchanging suitable pleasantries, Lady Jersey and Lord Merlin made their way back to the Jerseys' box.

"Ah, Sally, I am in your debt, " Merlin murmured.

She laughed. "Then you must come to Almack's yourself," she said. "That will be suitable payment for me."

"I shall be there," Merlin promised, if he winced at the idea of such a dull evening.

"She's a very fetching female, you know," Lady Jersey said lightly.

"Miss Dysart?"

"Heavens, no!" She looked at Merlin. "You are a very great rogue, Nick, and I think you've met your match at last!" She tapped him playfully with her fan. "Just be thankful that Emily Cowper likes you too, or I never could have procured those vouchers."

"I haven't the faintest idea what you're getting at, Sally," Merlin replied blandly.

Susan's cup was overflowing. She understood, from the Shelby sisters, how difficult it was to enter the sacred portals of London's most exclusive assembly rooms. But it seemed that her aunt's power could open any door.

The curtain rose on the play, and for the next hour, Susan was totally lost in the story that unfolded on the stage. Highly romanticized, the play presented Mary Stuart as young, lovely, and innocent, which

suited Susan's tastes perfectly. Madam Hart was
thrilling, heroic, and beautiful, the stuff of which a
young girl's daydreams were spun. There was a
handsome hero to play Darnley, and the sets and
costumes seemed to be conjured from magic.

She was so enthralled that she quite forgot to be
afraid of Lord Merlin, even when she saw him staring
across at their box rather than watching the play.
In fact, almost no one seemed to be preoccupied with
what was going on the stage, save Miss Dysart and
the Shelby ladies. People strolled about the theater,
talking over the actors' lines, visiting from box to
box, eating, laughing, and gossiping. From the pit,
the rowdies' cheers and catcalls echoed through the
theater whenever they were pleased or displeased,
and the orange girls peddled their fruit during the
actor's most dramatic speeches. Some boxes were
hired by what Giles called Covent Garden Abbesses
to show off their latest female acquisitions, and these
painted, flashily dressed women never missed a chance
to expose their charms to the bucks and rakehells
who were slumming from the stalls, ogling them
(and the ladies) through their quizzing glasses. The
celebrities in the royal box were fortunate that they
were stared out of countenance by the steady inspection
of the curious, who never hesitated to cheer or hiss
their betters, caught on the mood of the moment. It was
a large, noisily cheerful scene made noisome by the
smell of the limelights used to illuminate the stage
and the press of humanity in the building.

It was a testament to the actors' talent and profes-
sionalism that they could act at all in this bedlam,
let alone create the silver illusion of the theater. But
Emma Hart and company were troupers, raised up

in a harder school than London, and they carried on to the end of the second act, where Mary was imprisoned by Elizabeth. The lights dimmed and a chorus of singers and dancers spilled out on the stage.

The party, led by Lady Wellford, moved down the stairs and through the stage door. Behind the scenes, a chaos of sets, stagehands, spear carriers, dressers, wardrobe women, dancers, musicians, singers, actors, and managers moved quickly about on their business. The smell of greasepaint, sweat, and dust hung in the air. One or two dandyish fellows hanging about the scantily clad dancers looked as if they would like to ogle the ladies, but seeing Major Shelby's expression, quickly changed their minds and drew back to allow them to pass.

As befitted a great actress of her stature, Madam Hart enjoyed a large dressing room, furnished with a very grand dressing table, the surface almost completely covered with cosmetic pots, several large mirrors, portraits of the great tragedienne by Lawrence, Romney, and Hayter in the costume and attitude of her greatest roles, screens, chairs, a lounge, and, of course, Sir Peyton Rudge. An enormous number of floral arrangements provided by admirers of her talent, added their intense, hothouse scent to the musky atmosphere. Since Siddons had retired from the stage, Madam Hart was generally acknowledged to be the reigning Queen of the Boards. This was her throne room.

If the Great Tragedienne looked, upon close inspection, to be somewhat longer in the tooth and broader in the beam than the fairylike Queen of Scots she was playing, her admirers were too awed by the sheer force of her majestic personality to dare to even

think such thoughts. Having thrown off her wig and
ruff, draped by her hairdresser in an elaborate
embroidered dressing gown and attended to by her
entourage, Emma sat enthroned at that great dressing
table, being prepared for the final act. Coached by
Lady Wellford to mind her manners and her tongue,
Emma Hart played the role of gracious icon to the
hilt.

"Oh, Madam," Mrs. Shelby said, shaking her
hand, "I cannot tell you what a momentous thing
this for me. I have so long been an admirer of yours,
ever since I was a little girl and saw you as Juliet at
the Queen's Theater in Bath!"

Madam looked only a little pained at this, much to
her credit, and presented Mrs. Shelby with a copy of
her lithographed likeness as Lady Macbeth, which
very much pleased that lady, who went on to enumer-
ate the roles in which she had seen Madam over the
years. All of them, according to her, were triumphs
of the theatrical art, which slightly mollified the
tragedienne.

She was all that was gracious to the three girls,
coaxing them out of their awe, and allowed Giles to
kiss her hand.

Sir Peyton's stays creaked as he bowed over the
young ladies' hands, uttering fulsome compliments
of the sort that might have been expected from a
longtime intimate of the Regent. That he thought he
was the epitome of gallantry was quite obvious.
That Susan, Jane, and Emily were too young and
naive to fend off his increasing raillery with a polite
snub was suddenly obvious to Lady Wellford, who
quickly diverted her attention to him. His sensibilities
would have been severely wounded had he been

accused of vulgar cupidity. Mrs. Shelby, involved in conversation with Madam Hart, did not notice this subtle drama, but Giles, who had, was taking on a very ugly look indeed.

"I must say, Sir Peyton," Major Shelby exclaimed in a very nasty tone, stiffening his shoulders and doubling his fists.

"Giles, I'm sure that's not what Peyton meant—" Lady Wellford began. *All I need is this hotheaded young fool calling that poor old man out,* she thought rather desperately. *Then there will be scandal broth!*

Then Lord Merlin made one of his unexpected appearances. Beneath hooded eyes, he sized up the situation in a glance, and, casually stepping between the puzzled Sir Peyton and the about-to-be-offended Giles, he laughed. "Carrying on one of your flirts, Rudge?" he asked lightly, turning to the wide-eyed girls. "You must be careful of Sir Peyton! He is an enthusiastic connoisseur of female pulchritude and a hardened flirt who has broken many hearts."

This small jest, which carried no barb, served to diffuse the tension. Giles relaxed his stance, Sir Peyton smiled angelically, and the girls tittered appreciatively.

Audrey's sigh of relief was barely audible, but Merlin caught the flash of gratitude in her eye.

Sensing something, if not precisely what, had transpired, Madam Hart's sharp eyes cast over the little group. "Sir Peyton," she said in low tones to Mrs. Shelby, "is irresistible to females! They cannot resist him!" In her ringing theatrical voice, she called, "Ah, Lord Merlin! How very kind of you to come by!"

"I had no idea that you had other guests," he said, bowing over her hand in the expected obeisance.

"You know each other?" Audrey asked, much startled.

"I met Lord Merlin on my way out of your house this afternoon," Madam said complacently. "Naturally, I invited him to come and see me in the entr'acte."

"Naturally," Audrey said. She turned to look at Merlin. "So," she said in an undervoice, "Are you now reduced to lurking at my front door?"

"Better that than crawling out of a window," he said lightly in the same low tone. "Actually, you were occupied and I had a most pleasant stroll about your rose garden with Miss Fishbank, who is a female of remarkable good sense and discretion. You are fortunate to have her by you. Someone else might have raised a hue and cry at the sight of a young man in a hussar's uniform climbing down the ledge from your window into the terrace. Quite the athlete, ain't he?"

Audrey felt embarrassment. She could not quite meet Merlin's eye. "What do you want? I am certainly not going to encourage you, you odious man, to bedevil me or my niece!"

"What do I want? A very good question. I am as rich as any India nabob. I have inherited a title, which I sometimes find useful in procuring myself a better room in an inn or an invitation to some dull London party. I have a seat in the House, which affords me a certain amusement. I enjoy excellent health, and believe it or not, the company of some fine friends. I have a large house in town and a larger estate in the country. What else could I possibly desire?"

"I wouldn't presume to guess," Audrey replied stiffly.

"Then I will tell you, if you will drive in the park

tomorrow. Perhaps it is time we talked rather than fought with each other." He smiled, transforming his craggy features, "Besides, I am an admirer of your horseflesh and your phaeton! I should enjoy being driven by such a whip as you!"

"I might throw you," Audrey warned, but she found herself returning his smile nonetheless.

6

At five-thirty, Lady Wellford, attired in a bottle green driving dress, a Russian toque on her curls, swept through the gates of the park, driving her yellow-wheeled phaeton behind her matched grays.

Having left Miss Fishbank to chaperone Susan and the major on a sedate pedestrian ramble along the paths, she felt a slight sense of relief, as if she had been let out of a cage. Fond as she was of her niece, it was pleasant to have a few hours in which she did not have to supervise her comings and goings.

As annoying as Merlin could be, she had to admit that she was looking forward to hearing what he had to say, if only because it would not involve endless prattle about clothes, beaux, balls, routs, and parties where the famous were to be seen. Truth to tell, she was thoroughly bored with hearing the praises of Wellington, too!

It was with some relief that she saw Merlin, dressed with neatness, if not great fashion, in a tan jacket, black pantaloons, and topboots, strolling along the path. Only then did she realize she had half-thought he might not appear.

She pulled up beside him and told her groom to wait for her at the gate. In a moment, that stolid worthy was exchanged for Lord Merlin, who climbed into the vehicle with only a little grumbling about his ancient knees. "I wish," Audrey said sharply, "that you would leave off complaining about your ancient joints. You're only about eight years older than I am, Merlin!"

"That's a fine way to start the beginning of our truce," he remarked, watching her handling of the reins critically.

Audrey knew herself to be a good driver. "You needn't grip the seat and hiss through your teeth every time I take a corner. Wellford was a capital whip, and he taught me to drive through a narrow gate until I could do it without scratching the paint."

"I have no censure to make with your driving," he said gravely. "If you were a man, I would invite you to join the Four Horse Club!"

"If I were a man," Audrey repeated ruefully. "Sometimes, I wish I were a man! Then there would be fewer constraints upon me!"

"Ah, a follower of Miss Wollstonecraft? I would never take you for a bluestocking, you know."

"I've been known to read a book or two. Wellford and Appie both encouraged me to close the gaps in my education."

"He must have been an admirable man. I left for India before you married him," Merlin said thoughtfully.

"I was sincerely fond of Wellford," Audrey replied, letting down her guard a little as she thought of her late husband. "He was the kindest man I have ever known, and the wisest. I was fortunate. Many young girls who are sold into marriage are buckled to men with far less intelligence and sensibility."

"And your niece?" Merlin asked, his voice deceptively casual.

"I lacked her courage," Audrey replied. "It never occurred to me to do as she did. How could you have countenanced such Turkish treatment as Robert and that woman ladled out! Locking a girl in her room, feeding her on bread and water, and browbeating her ceaselessly about her duty to marry a man that she feared—well?"

"What?" Merlin's mocking stance evaporated. He seemed genuinely astonished. "Locked her in her room? Browbeat her? Come now, Audrey, this is the nineteenth century, not some Gothic tale from Walter Scott!" He looked at her expression. "You *are* serious, aren't you?"

"Never more so," Audrey replied. "You may doubt it, but I can tell you from my own experience that my brother is no stranger to the role of Roman parent! If I had not grown up at Bleakfriars, I would have doubted the tale Susan told me, too. But, you see, I *did* grow up at Bleakfriars." Briefly, she sketched what she had learned from Susan about the state of affairs that had driven the girl to run away.

"I had no idea. That is, I knew that Miss Dysart was somewhat in awe of me, but I attributed it to a natural shyness. Of your brother and Mrs. Dysart, well, you would know their character better than I. But this is not what I wanted—or expected! Good Lord, what a tangle! No wonder Miss Dysart—" He fell silent, and Audrey, stealing a sideways look at him, apprehended that he was thinking hard new thoughts. A muscle in his jaw twitched, and he drove his fists into his pockets, whistling tunelessly through his teeth.

"It begins to fall into place," he admitted at last. "I begin to see what was happening, now. Good Lord! Poor, silly chit! But how was I to know?" He laughed. "What a fool I must have looked, storming into your drawing room like that! But after what the Dysarts said about you, I was certain that I should have to rescue your niece from a den of iniquity!"

If Audrey was expecting an apology, she was disappointed, but hardly surprised. She doubted Merlin would admit he was wrong under torture. Men! Nonetheless, the discovery that he was ignorant of Susan's plight softened her attitude enough for her to feel slightly more civil toward him.

"You know," he added thoughtfully, "I never did like Robert. He was a sneaky boy, and he's grown up to be a sneaky man. Judging by the state of the place, I'd have to say that he's swallowed a spider and is up the river tick! The gossip in the neighborhood is that his wife is ruinous hard to keep up."

"That woman is a greedy, grasping witch!" Audrey started. "She would sell her own daughter to keep up her pretensions to gentility!"

"And I was the mark. Of course, I was willing to make a good settlement, pay off Robert's debts. You can't have the bailiffs in your in-laws' house, you know."

"I have decided that I will make a settlement on Susan when she marries," Audrey said carefully. "But she will not marry where she cannot be happy, and the money will be held in a trust for her use alone. I have seen far too many wives ruined when their money becomes the property of a profligate husband! I would not have it happen to my niece."

"Oh, no, of course not," Merlin said indifferently. Having acquired so much of his own while in India, he was indifferent to the fortune of a prospective spouse.

"I hope you understand that," Audrey told him. "But, since we are speaking so frankly, perhaps you can tell me what possessed you to offer for a young girl who is obviously terrified of you?"

"I don't see what makes her so afraid of me," Merlin said innocently. "I never tried to make violent love to her or anything of that nature. I tried to be civil, damn it! I told her from the start that once she had provided me with an heir, she was free to pursue her own interests, and I would pursue mine."

"You cannot be serious!" Audrey exclaimed. She laughed, shaking her head so that her plumes quivered. "Nicholas, you cake!"

"Why? What's wrong with that?" Merlin looked puzzled.

"Why, she's just a child! It would be quite different if you were offering for a woman with some experience and common sense, but to say such things to a mere child, and a romantical female at that, shows how little you know about women!"

"I see!" Merlin said meekly. "I thought she would be happy to be a viscountess and the mistress of a great pile like Merlinford and a townhouse like Merlin

House! It seemed to me that that was what the family wanted."

"What did you do, throw open all the state rooms and prose on about the duties of a viscountess?"

"Well, something like that. I thought the chit would be impressed." He scratched his head. "Damme, Audrey, I've been in India for the past fifteen years! Things are different out there! How in the devil's name am I to know how to court a young lady? Schoolroom misses are not precisely the sort of females I'm used to dealing with."

"A little civility would not come amiss! You must admit that your manners are abrupt, overbearing, and sarcastic, exactly the sort of thing that is calculated to terrify a young and naive female who has been stuffing her head full of novels and romantical notions."

"I stand corrected," Merlin said humbly. Audrey did not see the way in which his lips twitched, or the glitter in his eye; she was far too busy handling her team as she swerved to avoid a dowdy barouche in the road. "Then, if I wanted to pay court to a female, what would you suggest I do?"

"You might begin by paying a little attention to her," she suggested. "And by cultivating her acquaintance a little. You must admit that your manners are abrupt and highhanded."

"Whenever I look at her, she flies into a panic," Merlin admitted ruefully.

"And no wonder! You've terrified her! Viscountess and grand houses and scenes in people's drawing rooms. *And,*" she added, "you have a way of appearing at the most unexpected times and saying the most annoying things! What in the world were you doing watching Giles climb out the window, as if it was any of your business?"

"Oh, I just happened to encounter Miss Fishbank on the street. I mentioned how sadly neglected the rose gardens at Merlin House are, and she invited me to see what your gardener had done. Bone meal and manure, I believe, are sovereign fertilizer for roses!"

Audrey, who paid little attention to the gardens, and indeed, had a deep suspicion of anything to do with the out-of-doors, merely shook her head. "I do believe it's Miss Fishbank you're cultivating! It won't do you any good, you know. She has no influence at all over Susan!"

"None whatsoever," Merlin agreed cheerfully. "But she is an old friend of mine, so you cannot begrudge her my company. She feels, like the roses, sadly neglected since Miss Dysart came to stay, I fear."

That Appie's nose might be out of joint had never occurred to Audrey. "Ridiculous," she said firmly. "Appie is never out of sorts! The subject is my niece, if you recall."

"Oh, yes, of course." Merlin leaned back against the seat. He looked a little bored.

"And how you may overcome her resistance to your suit."

"Resistance. Yes, I suppose she is resistant. I think she thinks that I am entirely too old for her. Perhaps you could advise me upon that head."

Audrey threw him a sharp look. "We are not discussing my life, but yours."

"But yours is so much more interesting! All London is buzzing with the on-dit of you and your very young beau. Or at least they were, until all the foreign princes came to town."

"You know, you have always had a talent for saying precisely the wrong thing," Audrey said irritably. "I don't think Major Shelby is anything to do with you."

"Fine sort of fella! Strips to advantage, looks well on a horse, handsome as the devil in his uniform, and lands a bruising punch. Thing of it is, I have a little trouble imagining you following the drum. And the fella means to stay in the army. He won't sell out, you know."

"Nor do I expect him to! Major Shelby's career is not my affair. As I told you before, I have no intention of marrying again! Widowhood is the ideal state for a woman. She is free of the constraints the law and society place on spinsters and married women, and has her own money to do with as she pleases. She need answer to no man, nor any woman either! Since Wellford left me not only comfortable, but also fully instructed in the management of my finances, I have managed to contrive very well, thank you!"

"As you say," Merlin murmured. "Still, what if you were to fall in love?"

"Love?" The way Audrey pronounced the word made it sound faintly vulgar. A cold little smile played over her features. "How do you know that I am not in love with Major Shelby? Or the Tsar? The Regent? General Blücher? It seems that everyone is in love with General Blücher these days."

"It must be those great military mustaches. I heard that he fell asleep at dinner last night after consuming a great deal of wine. One minute poor Prinny was talking to him and the next, he was asleep in his *veau viennese*."

Audrey gave a little gurgle of laughter. "I can certainly not love a man who falls asleep at the dinner table. That would never do! No, I must needs place my hopes on the King of Prussia when he comes this week! Of course, since the Emperor of Austria declined to come, perhaps he would have been my best last hope!"

"He's quite the satyr, I understand," Merlin informed her. "He would chase you around the dinner table!"

"Prinny chased me around the Chinese Salon at Brighton once," Audrey recalled. "I of course said no. I was married to Wellford at the time, and young enough to be very shocked! Imagine having that great whale of a man puffing around after you! Now of course, I would laugh about it, but I assure that it was no laughing matter to me at the time. Fortunately, Mr. Brummel came into the room, or I don't know what would have happened next!"

"I should have liked to see you! No doubt you would have broken a vase over his head!"

Audrey laughed. "Hellfire and brimstone, no! That is, gracious no! My wretched tongue! Sometimes I think that I will never make a good chaperone."

"Truth to tell, I think you are handling the situation far better than I expected," Merlin said. "I have to admire the way in which you have managed Miss Dysart's launch."

Audrey smiled at the unexpected compliment and felt very much more in charity with her companion. "It is not easy, managing a green girl," she confessed. "Susan is a sweet-natured, biddable chit, but she has a mind and a will of her own." They drove for a while in a companionable silence, then she spoke again.

"Tell me, since we speak frankly, why you decided to offer for my niece? Surely, there have been a thousand girls thrown at your head since you inherited the title?"

"Never a thousand! Who do you take me for, the Duke of Devonshire?" Merlin sighed. "As you know very well, I have a duty to marry. Produce an heir, continue the line. I came back to Merlinford with no idea of management. My cousin did nothing to train me to replace him. As head of the family, I was forced to listen to m'grandmother and my aunts spell out to me in no uncertain terms that marriage is my duty. Miss Dysart was, well, near at hand."

"And That Woman was forever pushing her into your notice, I am sure. All very stupid," Audrey sighed. "Well, it sounds to me as if this courtship has been bungled very badly indeed."

"I'm not much in the petticoat line, as I said before," Merlin admitted.

"Well, you need to know how to go on, then." Audrey brightened a little. Perhaps, she thought, there was some hope yet that Lord Merlin could come up to snuff as a suitor. He had *potential,* she thought. He was attractive, in an irregular, masculine sort of way, she had to admit. His abrupt, amused manners were certainly no deterrent to attraction; no less a lady than Sally Jersey counted him as a friend, and *she* was a high stickler indeed. True, he could be arrogant and had a most deplorable sense of humor, but there was something about his commanding attitude that made a female feel as if he were equal to any challenge. And that could be counted as a bonus, if one were so inclined. She was forced to admit that, in spite of herself, she could appreciate Merlin's good qualities. But, in this new light, she was forced to consider an unexpected but hopeful thought. Given a course in beaulike behavior, would he do for Susan?

"So, tell me," Merlin said, breaking into her thoughts, "How does one make oneself an attractive suitor?"

This question seemed to Audrey to answer her own. He was, she concluded, still interested in courting her niece. If he could become a beau ideal, would Susan find him more appealing? If Susan could be enticed to give him a second chance, perhaps she would see what Audrey was coming to see in him.

Since she enjoyed managing other people's lives, the temptation to meddle in this situation was almost more than she could resist.

"Make yourself a little less frightening," Audrey advised. "Perhaps, if she has a chance to see you in more relaxed circumstances, she might find you a delightful companion. You can be quite charming, when you are so inclined."

"Thank you," Lord Merlin said meekly. "I shall try my best to continue to be so!"

"Shared interests are crucial!" Audrey instructed. "Although I really don't think Susan has any interests yet, except parties and gossiping with the Shelby girls and clothes and novels from the Minerva Press. Tonight, she makes her Court Presentation; tomorrow, we make our first appearance at Almack's. I will take her to Covent Garden to see *The Magic Flute* later this week. Catalani is singing, so the evening won't be a total bore. I hope you are not bookish, for Susan is decidedly not! Those novels are all she reads. As far as I know, she has no domestic skills; I had none when

I married. She is very young, you know, and did not have Appie as a teacher."

"What else should I do to make myself an attractive suitor?"

"Show consideration. Listen to what she says, and pay attention. Laugh at her jests, respect her opinions, even if you do not agree with them. The ideal beau *respects* one's sensibilities."

"Should I be taking notes? I forgot to bring a pencil or a notepad."

Audrey wrinkled her nose. "Do I sound so pedantic? Forgive me! But I have great many gentlemen for my friends, and to my mind, even the best of them are sadly lacking in those qualities that females find most appealing."

"Such as?" Merlin leaned forward, genuinely curious now.

"Affection, for one thing. Tenderness, for another. It is excessively odd, but men, unless they are trying to *seduce* one, almost never want to share their sensibilities with one. They pretend that they have no feelings, which leaves one always guessing. Why is it that men and women never seem to be able to *talk* to each other?"

"It would appear to an outsider that we're talking right now."

"Yes, but if I were to ask you what your *emotions* were, you would blanch! See, you are already looking distinctly uncomfortable."

"Very true." Merlin ran a finger around the inside of his stock. "But men are supposed to be silent, stolid, and strong! You females complain if we are not! Then, you complain that we have no sensibility. Only look at the females who are attracted to Wellington!

You would be hard-pressed to find a more taciturn, unyielding, emotionless block than the Iron Duke!"

"Well, there you have it," Audrey said. "It is every female's fantasy that she alone can break down those hard walls, I suppose."

"I don't understand females at all," Merlin sighed.

"Nor do I understand men!" Audrey retorted.

They looked at each other and both laughed There descended upon them a feeling of being much more in charity with each other than previously.

For the remainder of the ride, Merlin entertained her with tales from his Indian adventures. He was a droll storyteller and a shrewd observer whose travels through the subcontinent had led him into a great many exotic places. Audrey, for whom boredom was the greatest vice, never once lost her interest in listening. Unlike many females of his acquaintance, she was neither prudish nor squeamish, and he was refreshed to find that she had developed a superior understanding and a habit of taking an interest in events outside the narrow, gossipy world inhabited by the Upper Ten Thousand.

This she was able to ascribe to the early tutelage of Miss Fishbank. "She is a great believer in education for females," Audrey admitted. "She always says, 'If you adopt the habits of reading and listening, you will never be bored and you will never be boring'!"

"Very true!" Merlin replied. "But do we also owe Miss Fishbank for your marvelous transformation from that hoydenish, gawky miss in braids I remember to your present state as diamond of the first water?"

"Toadeater!" Audrey cried, but she was not displeased by compliments from so hard a critic. "You were a thoroughly nasty boy with a pocketful of stones and frogs, and you had spots!"

"We were quite a pair," Merlin reminisced. "It would have been hard to find a more unattractive pair of children than we were."

"Well, there *was* my brother."

"I can never quite forgive Robert for bearing tales of us to my uncle when we broke a window in the dining room with a cricket ball."

"Very typical of him!" Audrey sniffed. "Especially since *he* was the one who broke the window."

There was shared laughter.

"So," Merlin said after a moment, "do you believe I could become a suitable suitor?"

"If properly groomed," Audrey replied seriously.

He smiled. "I must of course, bow to your superior judgment in these matters."

"Oh, yes! I think I know what I am talking about. If you show your softer side, I have no doubt of your success. And of course, you must take pains with your dress. That jacket will never do, you know, for a beau."

"Thank you, Audrey," he replied humbly.

"Perhaps I misjudged him a little," she said later to Miss Fishbank and Susan as they had tea with the major in the sitting room on Half Moon Street. She was recounting their outing, with a little editing, to her interested audience. "He may not be as black as I had originally painted him."

Certainly, with her to guide him, Merlin had the potential to become a polished beau, she thought.

Her attempt to drop a hint into Susan's ear was not

as successful as she might have hoped. Indeed, the little group all seemed to be in a brown study. Giles was sullen, Miss Fishbank snappish, and Susan positively hipped.

"He only needs a little polishing, for when he exerts himself, he is extremely charming," she added. "Giles likes him, don't you?"

"Giles isn't being forced to marry him every time he turns around! He is *still* old and full of eccentric starts," Susan replied spiritedly. "You might find him worthy of being polished, Aunt, but I cannot!"

So saying, she excused herself from the room and all but ran out the door.

"I say, Audrey, that was clumsy!" Giles snapped.

"I stand corrected. Really, Giles, there's no need to bite my head off!" Audrey said pettishly.

"What's wrong with you, Audrey? Can't you see she don't want to marry Merlin?" Giles exclaimed. "Let me try to catch her—" His cup rattled on the table as he followed Miss Dysart out the door.

"Susan!" His voice echoed in the hall.

"Well," Miss Fishbank said dryly. Her needle darted in and out of her canvas, and the corners of her mouth turned down a little. "If you had any fears of furthering that alliance, that should put your mind at ease upon that head."

That thought had indeed crossed Audrey's mind, for she was a confessed manager of other people's lives. "Well, don't rule it out, Appie," she said lightly.

"Oh, I don't," Miss Fishbank replied. "I think that Merlin would make a fine husband for the right lady. You'll never catch him crawling out of a lady's boudoir window."

Audrey threw her a look, but Miss Fishbank's

expression was angelic. "You will catch him bursting into a lady's drawing room, however," she countered, and poured herself another cup of tea. "Really, Appie, what is wrong with everyone in this household of late?" she added seriously.

Outside there was a crackle of thunder, and a torrent of rain began to beat at the windows. Without warning, a summer storm had blown suddenly into the Metropolis. Miss Fishbank looked at the clock on the mantel. "Audrey, have you forgotten the time?" she asked, startled out of her usual complacency.

"Oh, Lord," Audrey sighed. "Not on the night I'm presenting the girls at Court! We'll all be drenched!"

By the time they were ready to depart for the Queen's Drawing Room that evening, Susan had cried profusely and apologized almost continuously for her outburst. She castigated herself as the greatest wretch in nature, an ungrateful creature who deserved nothing, let alone a full Court Presentation and vouchers to Almack's.

Audrey had accepted her apology the first time and forgotten the incident, devoting her full attention to the far more important matter of her own and Susan's Court toilettes.

Dress was no simple matter for any lady who wished to be presented to Queen Charlotte at one of the Royal Drawing Rooms. Nor could any lady fully feel that she was truly "out" in London Society without the all-important presentation.

Court dresses were enormous, cumbersome white gowns, heavily ornamented with beadwork and lace, caught up under the fashionably high waist with belts, and spread, in yards and yards of extra fabric, over hideous, old-fashioned hoops. They could weigh several stone, and be hideously uncomfortable. No lady could be without a headdress with at least five plumes and possibly more. Opera gloves and almost every jewel a female possessed completed this cumbersome, burdensome toilette. In addition, females had to stagger about on old-fashioned, high-heeled satin shoes fastened with diamond buckles. In fact, Wescott had brought out every diamond in Audrey's considerable collection for this evening, draping her mistress in a considerable parure of bracelets, brooches, necklace, earrings, and tiara.

Susan's Court dress had cost Audrey almost as much as the rest of her niece's new wardrobe combined, and her own, dragged out of storage from her own presentation several years before, had set the late Lord Wellford back many, many guineas. Both ladies' gowns looked like nothing more or less than elaborately iced cakes, but Susan, as befit a young girl in her first Season, was ornamented only with a wreath of white roses, a single pearl-and-diamond bracelet, a pearl necklace, and pearl-and-diamond ear drops. This parure was a coming-out gift from her aunt. Such a delightful surprise was greeted with renewed expressions of gratitude and exclamations of Susan's unworthiness to be the recipient of such bounty. Finally Audrey had to ask her to refrain from becoming a watering pot again to quell further outpourings. Fully preoccupied with her own struggle to complete the complex Court toilette, Audrey may have been a little more abrupt than she needed to be, but in truth, nothing bored her more than an evening at Court .

"I remember when my friend Fanny D'Arblay,

when she was still Miss Burney, had to become a lady-in-waiting to the Queen, she very nearly expired from ennui and etiquette!" Audrey recalled. "Believe me, there is nothing stuffier than Windsor!"

It took all of their own combined efforts, plus those of Miss Fishbank and the redoubtable Wescott and two housemaids, to rig themselves into these outfits, and by the time the last towering plume was fixed, Otterbine had twice announced that the coach was waiting at the front door for them.

With all the footmen and Audrey's coachman in full livery, the heavy old coach, used only for the very grandest events, waited for them at the front door. Otterbine, ever the efficient butler, had caused the awning to be strung up between the doorway and the coach, and Lady Wellford and her protégée were able to squeeze their hoops in, settle themselves against the plush squab seats, and sigh, without too many droplets of rain upon their costumes.

Susan had perked up a little with the excitement of her Court Presentation, and stared out the window all the way to Windsor, commenting upon the passing scene.

A fortnight in the Metropolis had not inured her to its charms, and Audrey was much amused by her enjoyment.

"This, my dear, is the price we pay for Almack's and your own ball," she told her. "It will be over soon."

"Oh, I hope not!" Susan said naively. "Everyone dressed so fine, and the Queen and the Royal Princesses! Do you think the Regent will be there?"

"I certainly pray not," Audrey replied devoutly.

Presently, Lady Wellford's carriage joined a long line of equally imposing vehicles at the entrance to the castle that slowly, very slowly, discharged their glittering passengers into the interior.

"Now, Susan, don't forget. When you are presented, you walk toward the Queen, make your curtsy—*like wheat before the wind!*—just as Miss Fishbank taught you, rise, and then, without turning, back away."

Susan bit her lower lip. "I'm a little nervous," she said.

"Everyone is, the first time," Audrey said soothingly. "But the old Queen is very kind, and very homely, and has many daughters of her own, so she is inclined to be kind and understanding to young girls. Only thank God that Caroline is not queen yet!"

"Will the Princess of Wales be there?"

"No, and for that we must be grateful, since she is the most extraordinary female, and not at all the thing! But Princess Charlotte might be there, and you will enjoy seeing her!"

By gossiping about the royal family, Audrey was able to while away time and keep Susan distracted from her nervousness. The fact that Mrs. Shelby was bringing out Emily and Jane tonight helped somewhat. Audrey wished that they had been able to travel here in the same carriage, but five women in Court hoops would never be able to fit into even the largest coach!

However, just as their coach jolted forward another step, the door was flung open, and Major Shelby, resplendent in his full dress hussar's uniform and very wet indeed, flung himself into the coach.

"I ran ahead to see if I could find you in the line," he said, tossing himself into a seat and shaking rain all over both ladies.

"That's a fine thing!" Audrey exclaimed impatiently.

"Now we are all three wet! Giles, you inconsiderate, odious boy, how could you?"

She attempted to smooth out her dress, without much success.

Giles, looking astonished that his bravado was unappreciated, gaped at her.

"Giles was only trying to be kind to us, Aunt Audrey," Susan said, reaching out and taking his hand. Giles's fingers closed around hers and they exchanged a look.

Susan's cheeks flamed with color, and she dropped her eyes to her lap.

Giles darkened, and withdrew his hand. "Sorry," he said gruffly.

"Only thought it would pass the time. This line's so damned long, pardon me, Susan."

Audrey, who had not noticed that they had slipped into first names, dug in her reticule for a handkerchief and dabbed at the water spots on Susan's gown, every bit the officious aunt on an official occasion.

"Perhaps I'd better take myself off," Giles murmured in a sullen voice, feeling very unappreciated indeed. As he bent to unlock the coach door, his dress sword caught at one of Audrey's lace overskirts, With a loud, rending sound, the border tore away from the skirt.

"Bull in the china shop!" Audrey wailed in dismay as she surveyed the damage. "Oh, Giles! Look what you've done!"

"Go! Just go!" Susan implored the puzzled major, who knew, from years of experience with two sisters, that he had committed a major tactical blunder. Without another word, he departed into the night, just as Audrey's coach jolted forward and two royal footmen, resplendent in red and gold livery, threw open the other door.

"Hellfire and brimstone!" Audrey cried, much to the interest of the two impassive young men. "What a bobbing block Giles can be!"

'He meant well, Aunt, and he adores you so!" Susan said in defense of the major.

They were assisted from the coach with great ceremony and proceeded beneath a red awning up the stone stairs into the palace. "There will be a maid in the ladies' cloakroom who can repair this rent," Audrey said, calming immediately, as was her wont. "You wait in the anteroom, and I will meet you there in a moment."

Susan did as she was bid, feeling very awed indeed by the grandeur of the castle staterooms. All around her, ladies in their white hooped dresses, glittering jewels, and towering plumes were surrounded by gentlemen, either in the glory of their full dress uniforms, with gold braid, medals, epaulets, and dress swords or in the old-fashioned embroidered greatcoats and satin knee-britches dictated by Court etiquette. Many of the Season's debutantes were being presented tonight, so Susan was not short of acquaintances, but she knew that she would remember this event all her life for the excitement and glitter of a brush with Royalty.

Audrey might laugh and condemn Court circles as dreadfully dull, but for a young girl up from the country, it was exciting indeed. She was joined in a few minutes by the Shelbys, Mrs. Shelby, Emily, and Jane all looking very serious and stately in their Court attire.

Upon hearing about Audrey's mishap, Mrs. Shelby

immediately went to see what assistance she could render in the ladies' cloakroom.

The major appeared at Susan's shoulder. Seeing him in the light of a thousand tapers, the illumination reflecting off his medals and braid, she could not suppress a little gasp at his virile splendor. Giles was easily the most handsome man present that night, and as he grasped her hand in his own, she felt the warmth of his touch through her gloves. He gave her a speaking look, so full of meaning that a bright flame appeared in her pale cheeks. Try as she might, she could not tear her gaze away from his. Giles's eyes glittered. They seemed to her to speak more than words.

"Ah, here you are!" At that moment, Audrey reappeared, the rent in her gown mended. She adjusted one of Susan's plumes and smiled as she looped her hand through Giles's arm. "Shall we go in?" she asked. "Poor dear, I should not have snapped at you in such a way! You must think that I am a gorgon, and you are quite right! Will you forgive me?"

Giles swallowed heavily. "Of course. I know how ladies are about their fripperies," he said. A new and unexpected perception had entered his cognizance. It was a thought so overwhelming that his understanding was completely engaged in its computation. Never one to study his own emotions, the character that had led him to feats of valor on the battlefield and in the Corinthian set now failed him utterly.

Audrey, however, barely noticed. For her, the evening was a performance to be gotten through, and Susan's was the premiere performance that would reflect well or ill upon her aunt.

It was a simple matter for Audrey to attribute Susan's

high color and glowing looks to the excitement of
this very grand moment in her career. Hours of careful instruction made certain that she had no cause to
blush for her niece's conduct.

Queen Charlotte herself, very old and very homely,
with several of the Princesses in attendance, was seated
on her dais in the Reception Room. The influence of
the old King, now mad and entirely confined by his
physicians, was felt in the room, at least by those who
remembered him.

One by one, the debutantes and the newly married
ladies were called, and one by one, they approached
her, knelt in a deep, backbreaking curtsy, rose, and
withdrew, walking backwards away from the throne.
One must never turn one's back on Royalty! It was a
tedious process for those who merely watched and
waited, and when it was at last over, and limpid food
and flat champagne were served, it was a relief to
almost everyone. The room was extremely crowded,
and the heat was stifling. More than one woman,
overburdened by an excess weight of clothing in the
torpid atmosphere, fainted. When at last the Queen
withdrew and everyone else could leave, an almost
audible sigh of relief rippled through the gathering.

There was a long crush as people waited for their
coaches to be drawn up to the door again. Caught in
the press, Mrs. Shelby and Lady Wellford were able
to spend a good half hour congratulating each other
upon having fired their charges off upon the opening
sally of the Season and planning the next evening's
attack upon Almack's. Now that the girls were presented at Court, they were officially launched into
their debutante season. Society could officially recog-
nize their existence, and with luck, a series of eligible

gentlemen could begin to court them. If the girls dreamed of romance, their mamas dreamed of money and position. Even a girl without a sizable dowry might marry well if she were a diamond of the first water; Society still talked of the legendary Gunning sisters, two penniless Irish beauties who had taken London by storm in the last century. One had married two dukes, the other had married a fabulously wealthy peer. People had stood upon chairs to see them as they passed by, so famous did they become.

Mrs. Shelby and Lady Wellford were commonsensical enough to realize their charges would never rival the Gunnings as great beauties of the age. But they were able to reassure each other that neither Susan nor Jane or Emily was a quiz, either. Certainly the girls were pretty and fresh and young, and there was no need to blush for their dowries. Both ladies agreed that the evening had been a success.

Neither Mrs. Shelby nor Lady Wellford took any particular notice of the way in which Miss Dysart and Major Shelby hung back from the rest, deep in conversation.

7

"*Almost* anyone *can be presented* at a Drawing Room," Audrey said as Wescott applied the curling irons to her niece's hair. "Only look at the jumped-up mushrooms and toadeaters trawling through last night. Now, Almack's Assembly Rooms, that's entirely different! Only persons of the highest ton may appear there! It is a great deal too bad that the Shelbys are full of influenza right now and cannot come with us. But the major, you know, has his own rooms in the Albany, and we may expect to see him tonight." Audrey ruthlessly suppressed the thought that without the Shelby sisters, Susan would shine all the more. It was unworthy, but pragmatic; and Audrey was nothing if not pragmatic.

If her niece looked just a little hollow-eyed, and her smile was thin, Audrey was able to attribute it to the excitement of her first official week as a debutante. With her own hare's foot and pot, she stroked a little rouge into Susan's cheeks.

"Now you look more the thing, " she said, stepping back to observe her handiwork. "You'll be the prettiest girl at the ball!"

And, Audrey thought, Susan did look lovely. Gowned in white gauze with a net overskirt of spider-web lace, trimmed at bodice and hem with garlands of white satin rosebuds, she shimmered when she moved. Wescott's expert hand had turned her dark hair into a mass of curls, upon which she had placed a wreath of pearls and rosebuds. Her feet were shod in white-and-ivory striped dancing slippers, and she carried an ivory fan with painted medallions. She wore pearl ear-bobs and a single gold-and-pearl bracelet.

Wescott clasped a single strand of pearls about Susan's throat and stood back to examine her own handiwork with what might have been a grunt of satisfaction in a less august person than the lofty dresser. Truth to tell, she was enjoying dressing a young person. It presented a new challenge to her skills.

Susan surveyed herself in the pier glass and smiled, her problems momentarily forgotten in the excitement of her first ball gown. "Oh, thank you," she breathed, smiling at Wescott. She turned this way and that, admiring herself. "I can't believe it's really me," she said in tones of wonder.

"Whatever success I have as a lady of fashion I must lay at Wescott's feet," Audrey acknowledged.

Lady Wellford was turned out to her usual perfection. Her dark hair was sleek, with only a few tendrils artfully escaping on her cheeks. She wore a headdress of gold gauze with a spray of feathers. Her ball gown was pomona green silk trimmed with deep ruchings of forest green velvet and gold net, cut low across the bosom and high on the sleeves, trimmed with lozenges of gold and velvet. She wore her diamond-and-emerald parure, and had draped a cashmere shawl across her shoulders. She hoped, with her tongue just a little in her cheek, that she looked respectable; she had no doubt that she looked fashionable.

"Oh, Aunt! How very lovely you look," Susan breathed in admiration of her elegant toilette. "I feel just like Cinderella, and you are the most elegant fairy godmother!" A tiny cloud crossed her face. "If only I deserved all your kindness!" she blurted out.

Audrey, feeling a bout of wretched excess coming on, tapped her smartly on the shoulder with her fan. "There, there! No watering pots, please! You know I can't bear that! You look lovely, and there is no need to thank me yet again. My thanks will be your happiness tonight, when all the gentlemen are flocking around you, begging to fill your dance card!"

Mr. Willis, guardian of the sacred portals of Almack's, bowed low when he saw Lady Wellford. "It has been a long time since we saw you here last, my lady," he said admiringly.

"Too long," Lady Wellford agreed pleasantly. As she introduced the lofty maitre d' to her niece, she cast a quick look about the room. Nothing, she realized, with a small inward sigh, had changed here, at least. The rooms were still dingy, smelling of dust and candle wax, with the worst dance floor in London. The same country dances and minuets were played by the same orchestra, and the same faces were much in evidence. Watching Mrs. Drummond Burrell's face contort into an interesting expression as that haughty Patroness beheld Lady Wellford at the door, she was almost certain that the old dragon was wearing the same gown. There was the same whist for penny stakes at the card tables, and the same watery orangeat and flat champagne, the same dreary little dribs and drabs of food that passed for supper. Even the addition of the Tsar and the King of Prussia, in town for the peace celebrations, could not quite ignite the ambiance. Royalty, if anything, was even duller than commoners!

She could feel the same dreadful boredom creeping over her and she forced herself to smile, wondering for the thousandth time what made Almack's vouchers the most sought-after ticket in Polite Society.

Just then, the Ladies Sefton and Cowper saw her, and fluttered toward them. "Audrey! I don't believe it! Is it really you?" Maria Sefton exclaimed. "Sally said you would be here, but I didn't believe her!"

"Audrey! My dear, of all people!" Emily Cowper cried.

Kisses in the air and wide embraces were exchanged, and Audrey introduced her niece, who made a pretty curtsy.

The Patronesses knew what was expected of them, and it was the work of an instant to introduce Susan to several hopeful-looking young gentlemen who were hovering about, waiting for a chance to place their names on her dance card. One of them, a likely fellow wearing the uniform of the Coldstream Guards, offered his arm, and Susan drifted away to make up the next dance.

"Come sit down where we can have a cozy gossip, Audrey! Sally Jersey said you would be here, but I told her not Audrey! We're far too slow for her," Lady Sefton said, leading Audrey to a seat on the side of the room. "What a taking girl! Nice manners, and she looks very much like you."

"She's Robert's daughter. I'm firing her off this season," Audrey replied. She settled down in full expectation of a long, dull evening along the chaperones' wall. Here, the dowagers kept a sharp eye on their charges, looking for the smallest infractions from their own or, better, other young misses on the marriage mart. Gossiping the dullest, most speculative gossip, sipping warm punch, the chaperones droned on and on. Their surprise in finding the dashing Lady Wellford among their number was probably the largest stimulation many of them had received in a decade, and there were twitters and whispers among their set.

Audrey's foot tapped to the music, but she forced her smile to stay on her face, and exerted herself to be as charming as she could. After all, these old tabbies would all have to have balls for their charges, to which Susan must be invited, just as they must be persuaded to accept invitations to her ball.

Being charming to those whose rules one has ignored or flouted for years, however, is hard work, and Audrey was genuinely grateful when one of Susan's partners took pity on her and brought her a glass of champagne. That Susan was enjoying a notable success made Audrey's job no more simple;

jealousy was engendered in more than one hopeful mama's breast that evening.

Nothing could have matched her relief when she saw Lord Merlin appear in the doorway just a few minutes before eleven.

"Five more minutes, milord," said Willis, "And I would have had to refuse you admittance. Rules are rules, you know, sir."

Lord Merlin was as elegantly dressed as any gentleman present. From the wings of his dazzling white neckcloth, tied in the fashionable Wellington knot, to the tips of his correct patent leather dancing shoes, he was a model of sartorial elegance.

"Major Shelby is not far behind me," he told Willis, surveying the room with a cool, detached glance.

"Hero of Spain or not, sir, if he's not here at eleven, he can't get in," Mr. Willis pronounced firmly.

"Exactly so," Lord Merlin drawled, and advanced into the room.

He was greeted by Ladies Cowper and Sefton, with whom he was a prime favorite, and immediately made his way toward Susan, who appeared in no way pleased to see him. "Oh, it is you, Lord Merlin!" she said, flushing up to the roots of her hair.

Taking her dance card, he scrawled a name. "Have no fear, little one! I mean you no harm," he murmured with a devilish smile. "In fact, I may do you a great deal of good! Look over my shoulder!"

As she did so, Miss Dysart's face broke into a smile. Looking a little out of breath, Major Shelby was edging past the august Mr. Willis.

She was not the only lady present whose attention was captured by the handsome major. Several other ladies were staring quite openly at him, too, attracted by his stunning looks.

Lady Wellford was not one of them. The smile on her face was taking on a masklike intensity as she listened to Mrs. Drummond Burrell describe, in exhaustive detail, a recent operation that supercilious female had endured in order to have a tooth extracted by the royal family's own dentist.

Nor did Giles's eye fall upon Audrey or any other hopeful lady. After a brief conversation with Princess Esterhazy, he immediately strode across the room and picked up Susan's dance card.

"I'm afraid Lord Merlin has engaged me for the last dance I had," she stammered.

"By Jove, he hasn't! Looks as if the fella's scribbled my name on your card!" Giles exclaimed, much puzzled. "Don't that beat all?" He showed her the card.

"Whatever can this mean? Oh, Giles, you don't think—" At that moment, the music commenced for a country dance, and Susan was swept away to make up the set by an eager young man.

"Major, let me introduce you to the Grand Duchess," Princess Esterhazy said, ruthlessly descending on him and bearing him away to meet the Tsar's platter-faced sister, who was simpering at him as if he were a particularly delectable sweetmeat.

"Forgive me, Mrs. Drummond Burrell, but I believe Lady Wellford has promised me this dance," Lord Merlin said, taking Audrey completely by surprise as he swept her out to the dance floor.

"I never thought I should be so glad to see you!" Audrey exclaimed once they were out of earshot. "But should I be dancing? Is that proper for a chaperone?

Heaven knows I don't want to set the old tabbies off, and just when I am being so good!"

"Your charm never deserts you," Lord Merlin said gravely, and Audrey laughed.

"Oh, I am sorry! But you have no idea how dull it is here! For the past three hours I have been *impaled* by the stares of some of the worst old tabbies in town. And I have had to be civil! Being civil to people you don't even like is the most awful thing in the world! My only consolation is that they have to be civil to me in return, and I know it's torturing that Drummond Burrell woman! Being a chaperone is so very dull, you would not believe anything could be duller, Merlin!"

"Try me!" He laughed, spinning her into the figures of the dance. "And don't say I didn't warn you, Audrey!"

"Yes, you did. But Susan is having a glorious evening! She's meeting a great many gentlemen! If you wish to fix your interest, you'd better work fast."

"Alas, Miss Dysart's dance card is full. Major Shelby, who came in just after I did, managed to secure the last dance."

"Giles is here? But he never even came near me! How vexing that boy can be sometimes! Leaving me to rot from boredom while he capers around the dance floor."

Merlin's eyes glittered. "You will allow me to escort you in to supper," he said.

"Of course, and thank you for it." It was beginning to dawn on Audrey that Merlin was a fine dancer, and since she enjoyed dancing very much, she gave herself over to the pleasure of being his partner. "Oh, Merlin, I *should* not be dancing! I am, after all, a chaperone!"

"I doubt very seriously that Miss Dysart can come to any harm on the dance floor at Almack's," Merlin replied.

"No, I suppose not! But you are not helping matters by whisking me away from the chaperones, you know."

Merlin shrugged. "If a beautiful young widow having a dance with an old friend is improper, then Almack's is even stuffier than I had previously believed."

"Flatterer! If it is this widow and this 'old friend,' then perhaps we are in the suds."

"I'm so glad to see you dancing, Audrey!" Maria Sefton called as she tripped past in the arms of a gallant. "I would like to see you waltz!"

"There! You see! Maria has given you her blessing! You are rescued from opprobrium by the smile of a Patroness. And, I might add, given the all-important permission to waltz with me!"

With that, Audrey must be content, and she was. Several other gentlemen, encouraged by Merlin's example, approached to ask for dances also, and by the time she and Merlin went in to supper, Audrey was almost out of breath.

Susan and Giles were already seated at the table. Giles rose as Merlin seated Audrey at the table. "Dear Giles, thank you for escorting Susan into supper," Audrey said. "Are you enjoying yourself, Susan?"

"Oh, yes," her niece answered. "Giles has been most attentive."

"Very nice evening," Giles said stiffly.

Audrey looked at Giles's expression and read it to mean that he was sulking because she had been dancing with Lord Merlin. She touched his hand lightly. "You will forgive me if I don't waltz with you, won't you, my dear?" she asked. "It might cause tongues to wag." It was a great deal too bad, she thought, that she had been neglecting him so badly of late. If he felt as if he were being ignored, he did tend to get sadly out of sorts!

"Are the lobster patties edible?" Merlin asked blandly as he seated himself opposite Susan.

She started as if he had struck her, then, with an effort recovered herself. "I think so," she replied in a low voice.

"Giles," Audrey said quietly, bending close to him. "I know that I have not been as attentive to you as I should be of late. But you do understand, do you not, that so much of my time must be devoted to Susan right now?"

Giles looked down at his plate and nodded. "Yes, yes, of course," he said and reached for his champagne glass, which he drained in a single draught. "Don't worry about me—I'm the last one you should think about!"

"Oh, hellfire and brimstone, Giles," Audrey sighed. This air of martyrdom suited him ill, she thought impatiently. Nonetheless, she smiled and applied herself to charming him.

Lord, she thought as she smiled and fluttered her eyelashes, *if I keep this pace, I will be so thin spread of charm that the light will shine through me!*

For his part, Lord Merlin seemed to be having better luck with Miss Dysart. He had whispered something in her ear that seemed to make her lose her dread of him, for she smiled and the flame disappeared from her cheeks.

By the time they were joined by Lady Cowper and a jovial party, it seemed as if Susan was quite in charity with Lord Merlin, or at least so much so that she did not shrink when he addressed her, but was able to respond with a smile and a semblance of civility.

Witnessing this made Audrey feel considerably more hopeful of an eventual outcome. An outcome, she devoutly hoped, that would ensure that she would never have to eat dry roast beef and drink flat champagne and sit in the chaperone's corner again after this season. She was very grateful indeed that Merlin had come. If not for him, it would have been a dull evening indeed.

Surely, she thought, *he must indulge himself in a* tendre *for Susan if he was willing to subject himself to an evening of tedium at Almack's.*

She had a very strong feeling that only a sense of purpose could persuade Lord Merlin to appear at Almack's.

But when she said this to him as they waltzed about the floor, Merlin merely raised an eyebrow. "Ah, if you think that I would inconvenience myself this much for anyone, you are very much mistaken, my lady! I very much enjoy Almack's!"

With this reply, she had to be content. Seeing that she was dancing, the Tsar, who had an eye for pretty, sophisticated ladies, begged an introduction, and it was not long before Audrey had danced with almost every gentleman in the foreign entourage.

It was quite a while before Giles could find an opportunity to ask Audrey to dance.

"Audrey, we must talk," he said earnestly. "Things have progressed to the point where I can no longer remain silent."

"Yes, Giles! I know we must," Audrey said. "But not here, not right now, my dear. I know I have not been attentive to you recently, but believe me, I am thinking about you."

Giles somehow did not look gratified by this. But Audrey smiled and smiled. "I have hopes that my niece might begin to find Merlin's suit not unattractive. If I can but get that managed, then you and I will have all the time in the world."

"That's what I need to talk to you about. Audrey, I think—"

"I know! Say no more! I have become dull and respectable and you are bored to death with me. Oh, my dear, it is only for a little while, and then we will be together again. But for now, I must put all my heart into Susan's launching."

"Oh, Audrey, it's not that! " Giles said, exasperated. "I'm trying to tell you that—"

At that moment, the dance ended and the applause began.

"Perhaps we ought to step out on the balcony," Audrey suggested. "And have a breath of fresh air. This heat and excitement seems to have gone to your head, Giles. And I know I would like a glass of orangeat."

The balconies at Almack's were little more than small footholds with wrought iron balustrades outside the French windows. Once outside, Audrey breathed in the cool night air gratefully. Inside, she heard a pair of voices discussing—her.

"Can you believe it? Lady Wellford at Almack's! What is the world coming to, when the likes of her can get a voucher?"

"I'm sure I don't know! They say as how she's shooting her niece off into Society! I heard that she had to beg Lord Merlin to ask Sally Jersey for vouchers! Merlin, of all people! Can you imagine? She's worked her wiles on him, that's for certain. And then, her lover appears here, too! Pity about Major Shelby! He's a handsome lad, from a good family!"

"Can you imagine? But I had heard the only way she could procure entrée was to ask Lord Merlin to intercede for her with Sally Jersey! Outrageous!"

"Oh, well, there you have it! She's connived with Merlin to pull the wool over Sally's eyes, that's what it is! I wonder what she had to do to get him to take up for her? It's disgusting, that's what it is! I don't know what Society is coming to!"

As the voices drifted away, Audrey squared her shoulders, clenching and unclenching her fists. She minded little what people said about her. Shocking the ton had long been a favorite sport of hers. But for anyone to think Merlin had to intercede with anyone for her—that stung. Audrey, whose greatest pride was her confidence in her ability to live independently!

When Giles appeared with the orangeat, Audrey rose to her feet. "Do you know," she said, " I really feel like dancing!"

8

"*It says here that the Grand* Duchess, saying 'she has a morbid horror of music, requested the musicians be stopped at the Guildhall Banquet,'" Miss Fishbank said, reading from the *Morning Post*. "It rather pointedly adds that the Corporation of London had not invited her to the banquet, but she insisted upon coming. 'The Regent appeared greatly discomfited.' As well he might! 'When the Royalties appear in public, the Tsar and the King, as well as Generals Plutanoff and Blücher, are roundly cheered, but H.R.H. encounters only the hisses and jeers of the masses.' Dear me! 'It is widely believed that the King of Prussia has been asking to meet with Princess Caroline, his cousin.' After that incident at the opera, well he may!"

"What can you expect from that platter-faced

woman?" Madam Hart asked. "Audrey, I must have your chef's receipt for these chocolate comfits." To demonstrate her enthusiasm, she popped another one into her mouth, and with a gusty sigh, settled down among her shawls and scarves on the chaise beside the fire, where a comfortable heat permeated the damp London day.

Audrey, who had been looking out the window at the darkening clouds, scanning the rooftops for signs of a sunbeam, shrugged. "Of course, if you like," she said. "Ask Otterbine, he will be happy to procure it for you." She turned back into the room, hobbling on aching feet to a chair by the fire. "I don't remember dancing this much before, but I must have, somewhere down the line! I wore through a pair of slippers last night, and Susan wore out two."

From upstairs there was a thump, and she looked up at the ceiling. "At least it seems like she and the Shelby sisters have found an occupation for a rainy day. The girls seem to be quite over the influenza, but Mrs. Shelby is down now, poor dear! They're in Susan's room telling each other's fortunes with a deck of cards they found at the Pantheon Bazaar! Emma, have you ever been there? It's the most amazing place! Why, you can buy stockings for two and six, and an ell of India muslin for a shilling! It's a wondrous place for bargains!"

Madam Hart smiled. "Those of us whose fortunes are not unlimited know the Pantheon quite well. It's a wise woman who knows how to find a bargain."

"A friend of Mrs. Shelby's told her about it. I had my doubts of course, but once we were there, I went quite wild and bought quite a few things! Gloves at a guinea! Of course, I will end up giving about half of it to Wescott, but it was excessively diverting!"

"'Rumor has it that the Princess of Wales will cry off from her engagement with the Prince of Orange. He is insisting that she live in Orange when they are married,'" Miss Fishbank offered. She made a tsking sound.

"Quite right of her to do so, too," Madam offered. "We can't have the Heiress living abroad, you know!"

"It would seem she agrees with you. What a peculiar girl she is, to be sure! She bodes fair to resemble her mother."

"Well, she's had a peculiar upbringing, that's for certain. Prinny is quite the Roman parent where his own daughter is concerned. But I mean to keep him away from Susan! He still fancies himself Prince Florizel."

"Heavens, Audrey! All his *chères amies* are fat, fair, and forty! Susan's too young and too thin for his taste!" Emma said knowledgeably.

"It doesn't signify! A fine aunt I would be to allow her anywhere near that Carlton House set! Quite sunk below reproach!"

She looked out the window again, but the street was gray and wet and empty as it had been before. Not even a drayman's cart disturbed the silence. She found herself tapping impatiently on the arm of the chair but could not, for the life of her, understand why she felt so restless.

"'The son of a noble marquise is said to have lost thirty thousand pounds playing faro at White's last week.'"

"I know who that is! Peyton told me! It is only a great deal too bad that Peyton did not win that amount from him!" Madam remarked. She ate another comfit. "See if there's anything in there about a certain viscount paying particular attention to an opera dancer from Covent Garden."

Audrey looked up. "What viscount?" she asked sharply.

"Not Lord Merlin, if that's who you're worried about," Emma said indifferently.

"Of course I'm not!" Audrey rose and paced to the window again. "Will this rain *ever* end?" she asked. "Merlin! The very idea! Why, we haven't seen him here in a fortnight."

"'Lady S——— is said to have cut Mrs. D——— dead at a recent rout on account of both ladies' interest in the poet B———,'" Miss Fishbank read. "Oh, my goodness! And her not married above a twelve-month!"

"I find Lord Byron decidedly dull," Audrey said. "And his scandals are probably self-manufactured to keep his name in the public eye."

"Be that as it may, but did you hear that he—" Madam's voice dropped to a whisper, and even Audrey, who considered herself unshockable, gasped.

"Now *that* is a vile rumor!" she exclaimed. "Put about, no doubt by Caro Lamb. Since Byron threw her over, nothing seems too low for her. I think she's dicked in the nob."

"Audrey! What language!" Miss Fishbank reproved. "She's mad, poor thing."

"Well, that's what I said, Appie!" Audrey teased. "What else?"

"'The Duke of Wellington continues to attract large crowds wherever he goes. The adulation of the Great Hero seems to know no bounds. When he appeared in Hyde Park yesterday, he was overwhelmed by the press of persons wishing to see, or even touch him. Nor has the enthusiasm for the vulgar diminished for General Blücher, who can go nowhere without great cheers and accolades from the multitude.'"

"Well, let's see how the merry party does in Oxford this week. There's some sort of a go for them there, which seems to have pulled everyone out of town this week."

"If I never see another illumination again, it will be too soon for me," Audrey sighed. "And I used to love fireworks, too, until Prinny took to setting them off almost every evening in the parks. There's not a drop of fresh milk to be had! All the cows in Green Park are off their milk from the noise and excitement."

There was another thump from upstairs. "I wonder what they find in their futures?" Miss Fishbank asked. "Girls at that age see the world before them. Anything is possible, or so they think."

"I wish I believed that now," Audrey sighed, throwing herself into her chair. "Although I would not go back to that age for anything in the world."

"Beaux, clothes, parties," Madam Hart said complacently. She extended a hand and admired a new, and very large, diamond ring on her finger. "No, I enjoyed my youth thoroughly. But now, it is time for me to consider my retirement from the stage."

"What? It is as hard to imagine London theater without Madam Hart as to imagine the Regent without his stays," Audrey said, sitting upright. "But Emma, you can't be serious!"

"Oh, but I am, my dear Audrey. This will be the last season you will see Emma Hart tread the boards.

And it's time, you know. The ingenues get younger every year, and I do not. Best to exeunt, stage left, in triumph, than to hang about until one is reduced to playing character parts, crones and mothers."

"But what will you do without the stage?" Miss Fishbank asked.

"Emma, the theater has been your life!"

"Sir Peyton and I are thinking of becoming Beatrice and Benedick; in short, we plan to marry." Emma Hart said quietly. For her, *quietly* was a lessening of the dramatic tones of her famous voice. Nonetheless, she was smiling.

"What? You saved this news all afternoon and not a word?" Audrey asked, much astonished. "But Emma, how will I go on without you—that is, I wish you both well," she concluded, a little lamely, trying to avoid Miss Fishbank's disapproving eye. The sense that her friendship with Emma would forever be altered by marriage could not help but prey upon her mind. Nonetheless, she remembered her manners; she was not so selfish as to wish her friend ill. "I am sure you will both be happy. So that's the occasion for that big diamond ring!"

"Well, it will cause a nine days' wonder in London, of course," Madam Hart said calmly. "And you can depend upon it, Peyton's family will not like it above half, his getting buckled to an actress! It will set tongues to wagging, that's for certain. But we've been together for almost fifteen years now, and I've got a yen to make an honest man of him." Her eyes sparkled a little at her own joke. "We've been thinking about going to Paris, now that there's peace. Peyton hasn't been there since his Grand Tour, and I've never set foot out of England. So it will all be new to me."

"But Paris is so far away!" Audrey wailed.

"Yes, but you will come and visit us. Everyone is flocking to Paris now that there's peace, so you will be quite fashionable!"

"But Paris is where people live when they're not quite the thing!" Audrey said, upset.

Emma gave her a level look. "Oh, come now, Audrey. Actresses aren't quite the thing, as you and I both know. But, then, neither is Peyton, and we've got a mind for Paris. Besides, Peyton says the chocolates there are something to live for, so I imagine I shall enjoy it very much."

Audrey heard Miss Fishbank congratulating Emma upon her forthcoming marriage, but she felt as if she had been dealt a blow. Emma had been her dearest friend through most of her widowhood, and she knew that without her to pick it all over with, her life would be considerably duller.

"Won't you wish me well, Audrey?" Emma asked her quietly.

"Of course I do, and Peyton, too! You know that I am sincerely fond of him, and I know that he has always done everything in his power to make you happy—you have more jewels than Queen Charlotte, and—"

"And better ones, too. You might not believe it, but I'm a warm woman, Audrey. I've invested wisely, and never dipped deep, the way some of these young actresses do! I've the freehold of several good properties in the City. So, between the two of us, I daresay Peyton and I shall live exceedingly well in Paris."

"But will you be happy?"

"Happy? Of course I'll be happy. I love Peyton,

Audrey, and he loves me. Why else would we marry? We're both ready to settle down."

"But what about your independence? You always prized that as much as I!"

"It's not a question of independence, Audrey," Emma explained patiently. "It's wanting to be with someone always. It's love."

"Whatever makes you happy, Emma," Audrey finally said. "But I shall miss you a great deal."

Madam Hart laughed. "Oh, I have a feeling when you have the little one safely buckled, you'll be on the next packet boat to Calais! I can't picture you living one more minute than you have to without the latest French fashions! And of course, Peyton and I shall know all the great places to go. You'll see."

"It will make a fine excuse to come and see you," Audrey agreed, but she remained unreconciled. "When do you plan to marry?"

"At the end of the Season. And quietly, mind you, so there can be no gossiping about this! Peyton's procuring a special license. We'll be married at Saint Pancras' in the morning and be on the Dover packet by nightfall. If Peyton's sisters hear about this, they'll enact such a scene of fainting and carrying on as I've never played on the stage! I've yearned for years to see those two harpies put in their place." She grinned. "Imagine, Emma Hart of Bower Street becoming My Lady Rudge and living in Paris!"

"Yours has been a long and interesting career," Miss Fishbank said. "I'm sure that I wish you and Sir Peyton many happy years together."

"Well, you'll be coming to the wedding, both of you! I couldn't possibly be married without you as my witnesses. It will be very small—just a few close friends, and a wedding breakfast at the Piazza!"

"Knowing you, it will end up being a theatrical production," Audrey teased her.

"Very probably," Madam Hart agreed cheerfully.

At that moment, Otterbine entered the room. "There is a gentleman caller, my lady," he said.

Audrey looked brightly at the door, hoping that—

Then, as Otterbine ushered in Sir Peyton, she felt a sinking that she tried hard to conceal.

Sir Peyton was, as always, resplendent. His collar was so high that he could barely turn his head, and his neckcloth was tied in elaborate folds that cascaded over his splendid embroidered vest, featuring Chinese flowers and birds. He looked about the room and bowed to the ladies present.

"I take it my dearest one has informed you of our decision?" he asked, his stays creaking as he eased his bulk into a chair, leaning heavily on his gold-headed walking stick.

"Yes, and we are all agog with the news!" Audrey informed him. She nodded to Otterbine and the butler disappeared in search of Madeira and biscuits.

Sir Peyton nodded ponderously. He and Madam Hart gazed fondly at one another. "My little sparrow," he said fondly, "has agreed to do me the great honor of becoming my wife. I am the happiest man in London, what?"

"We are to offer you our felicitations, sir," Miss Fishbank said gravely.

Madam Hart reached across Sir Peyton's considerable bulk and patted his arm affectionately. "You are still my Apollo," she told him.

The sight of these two middle-aged people cooing at each other in terms of the greatest affection left

Audrey torn between amusement and something that would have felt suspiciously like jealousy to someone less strong in character.

She was heartily glad when Otterbine, bearing a tray of wine and food, entered the room and broke the spell.

"You'll stay to tea?" Audrey had only to ask.

Otterbine, seeing which way the wind was blowing, signaled one of the footmen to slip below stairs for more provender. Sir Peyton's appetite was as prodigious as his fiancée's.

"You may send a tray upstairs to the young ladies," Audrey told Otterbine. "I'm sure they would like some schoolroom fare on a rainy day like today."

Sir Peyton enjoyed a great many cucumber-and-watercress sandwiches, a good half-bottle of Madeira, and two plates of macaroons. Since his gossip, direct from Carlton House, was as prodigious as his appetite, he kept the ladies thoroughly entertained throughout teatime.

Yes, it was true about the Grand Duchess, and, yes, she was abominably platter-faced, and ill-mannered into the bargain. She had actually said, at the Guildhall Banquet, that music made her nauseous. It had been a most trying evening for poor Prinny, who had disliked her on sight. Nothing she had done since their initial meeting had revised his opinion. If she were not the Tsar's sister, no doubt Prinny would have given her a sharp set-down by now.

In addition, the Regent was plagued by his daughter, who was absolutely balking at becoming engaged to the Prince of Orange. She refused to live in Holland, and he refused to live in England. A queer, horse-mad girl, very blunt-spoken and abrupt! But when you considered her extraordinary upbringing, well! There you had it! Neither the Regent nor his estranged wife, Princess Caroline, were precisely ideal parents.

And had they heard that H.R.H. would apply again to Parliament to increase his allowance? The cost of the victory celebrations, added to all his other debts, had quite run him off his feet! Again!

Add to that the scandal broth that General Blücher had lost £20,000 or more in deep play with the deep gamesters at Carlton House, and you had a pother indeed. And had they heard that he had visited Mrs. Fitz in Richmond again? The Regent had thrown himself at her feet and wallowed about on the floor, and there had been tears and recriminations on both sides. Apparently the couple were reconciling again, although no one could guess the outcome, what with Lady Hertford breathing fire at Brighton!

Audrey, who ordinarily enjoyed Royal gossip, began to feel as bored as she had at Almack's. A few times, she found her gaze wandering toward the deep French doors that faced out on Half Moon Street, as if she expected to see—what?

In truth, she could not tell.

However, when Otterbine announced Lord Merlin, she felt a quickening of excitement and smiled broadly when that gentleman entered the room, still shaking raindrops from his hair.

He must greet all the ladies present, give his hand to Sir Peyton, offer his congratulations on the forthcoming marriage, refuse the offer of tea, and accept a glass of wine before taking a seat and throwing one long leg over the other, proclaiming in his gruff way that he could not stay long.

"I have come to offer you and Mrs. Shelby carte blanche for your ball at Merlin House," he told Audrey. "I have instructed my staff to offer you every cooperation. Unfortunately, I have been called to Merlinford on business, and there's no telling when I'll be back to town. I fear I have already neglected several matters of business there which need my attention."

Audrey was aware of a twinge of disappointment. "But you will be back in time for the ball?" she asked. "It would look very queer if the host were not there."

Lord Merlin smiled. "I certainly hope so! But no one who knows me will think it odd if I am not there. There are advantages to having a reputation for being odious and abrupt," he said, grinning.

"You wouldn't!" Audrey exclaimed, exasperated.

"I would do anything to get out of the way of a pair of females who will very likely drape my ballroom and my house in pink satin!" Merlin said frankly. "Experience has taught me that when the females are planning an entertainment, the gentlemen should best stay out of the way!"

"Exactly right, dear boy. I'd as soon face Napoleon's cannoneers as females planning a grand ball! Damned dangerous!" Sir Peyton nodded wisely. "Best thing you can do is show up on time in evening clothes and do as they say!" he advised.

"I think you are being excessively selfish!" Audrey cried, much put out. "You know very well that Charlotte Shelby and I can't just march in and start ordering your staff about!"

"All you need to do is give your orders to my steward; he'll take care of the rest. Believe me, he will be delighted to assist you in any way he can! I fear he finds employment under an unreconstructed bachelor deadly dull and hardly worthy of his skills. Believe me, he is as anxious as you are to blow off my consequence and make use of my ballroom."

"I still think you are being odious, Merlin," Audrey said, quite out of sorts.

"Audrey!" Miss Fishbank said reprovingly. "Lord Merlin is being extraordinarily kind in offering you and Mrs. Shelby the use of his house! There is no need for you to demand he do anything more, particularly when he has told you that he has pressing business at Merlinford."

Audrey had the grace to blush, but since this provoked laughter from Lord Merlin, she grew even more frustrated.

"A crimson flush upon those cheeks! Why, Audrey, I thought you said you were unshakable!" he teased her, knowing full well what her reaction would be. "Before she can comb my hair, I'd better leave," he informed the company. "Town life! It's not for the faint-hearted," he remarked. "My felicitations, Madam Hart, Sir Peyton! As always, your obedient servant, Miss Fishbank! Audrey, I shall leave you with carte blanche to wreck your revenge upon me by painting Merlin House purple or something equally outrageous!"

And with that, he was gone.

"And just when I was beginning to feel very much in charity with him!" Audrey, aware that he had managed to annoy her again, fumed after he had left.

Madam Hart laughed. "There, there, Audrey! Merlin always puts out the bait and you always bite! No need to take a pet, he's only being a man!"

"And a most sensible man at that! Would you really want him underfoot while you and Charlotte Shelby are dealing with florists and caterers and vintners and musicians and what-all?" Miss Fishbank asked with a great deal of common sense.

"No," Audrey admitted. "But it is most vexing of him to leave town just now when it seemed as if things are going so well between him and Susan!"

Madam Hart and Miss Fishbank exchanged a look.

"Merlin and Miss Dysart?" Sir Peyton asked, incredulous. "But I thought—"

"Have another macaroon, Peyton, my love!" Emma said quickly.

It was still raining when Lord Merlin left Half Moon Street, and he almost collided with Major Shelby, who was walking up the pavement, swathed in his cloak.

"Couldn't get a chair in this weather," the major said. "Had to walk." He glanced up at the windows of Lady Wellford's house with something akin to a moonstruck look.

The suspicion, which had been forming in Lord Merlin's mind for quite some time, that the major didn't have enough sense to come in out of the rain, was confirmed. It was his lordship's feeling that those who performed wartime heroics, like the major, were often lacking in just that sort of understanding. Doubtless, the man would have stood outside in the wet, gazing up at the windows in a sort of tortured longing for as long as a quarter of an hour and think himself a very romantic fellow for it.

"See, here, Shelby," he said, struggling to wrest the

Major's attention away from the windows, "I think you and I need to have a word, old man."

The major transferred a watery blue gaze from the windows to the countenance of the viscount. "I knew it would come to this! You want to call me out!" he said, thrusting out his handsome jaw. The effect was somewhat altered by droplets of rain water dripping from his fine military mustache. "I shall name my seconds, sir. Couple of fellows down the barracks will stand for me!"

"Don't talk fustian," the viscount advised him, not unkindly. "Why should I want to call you out?"

"Why, because of Susan—Miss Dysart, of course," the major said. He squinted at Lord Merlin. "D'you mean you don't want to marry her, sir? Then what *are* your intentions toward the lady?"

"Oh, for God's sake, man, are you foxed?" Merlin asked impatiently. "It's not even six o'clock!"

"I am a trifle beneath the gate," Giles admitted sheepishly.

"Go home and sleep it off!"

"Haven't been to bed from last night. Damn, Merlin, if you was in my situation, you'd be drunk, too! Not that it does any good, mind you. I just come and stand beneath her window and gaze upwards."

"I can't think of anything more revolting. Consider yourself fortunate that the watch hasn't hauled you in! Standing beneath a lady's window in the rain staring like a rustic doesn't solve anything, you know!"

His groom, who was walking Merlin's team up and down the street, called to him, "Best we head in, my lord! This damp ain't doin' the horses no good by half."

"You're right, Omber! Come, Shelby, let me take

you back to your lodgings. You need to get yourself on the level, friend!"

"Can't get on the level!" the major said gloomily. "In the devil of a pickle!" Nevertheless, Giles allowed Lord Merlin to assist him into his dashing Italian curricle, where he fell back in despair against the squabs, the very picture of handsomeness in abject misery.

If Lord Merlin were a man of sensibility, which he was not, he would have felt very sorry for Major Shelby. Instead, he said in bored tones, "I thought you were a downy 'un!"

"So did I!" Major Shelby sighed. "'Til *females* came into the picture! I've been thinking, Merlin, and I've decided females are a mystery! Tell me, Merlin, *what am I to do?*"

"I haven't the faintest idea, my boy. I thought all was progressing swimmingly. She is not, I think, indifferent to your suit?"

"Who?"

"Are we not discussing the lovely Miss Dysart?" Merlin asked patiently.

"She is lovely, isn't she? And not just on the outside, either. She's lovely through and through!"

"And true blue," Lord Merlin murmured wickedly.

"What? Oh, no, we're completely agreed on politics, as on every other head! She's pluck to the backbone, that one! Only think, she climbed down a drainpipe and—"

"Speaking of climbing down windows, my dear fellow, didn't I see you exiting from the boudoir of another lady not more than a month ago?"

"The point exactly! Well, no, not the point, actually. That is, well—things between Audrey and I never reached The Pass," the major mumbled, a little embarrassed. "Appearances to the contrary. That was when I was an impetuous boy and didn't know any better! I thought I was being romantical! Now that I'm really in love, I know better!"

"Ah," Lord Merlin said understandingly.

"Well, I *thought* I was in love with Audrey—but it turns out to have been something—well, not that she's not a beautiful woman, a lady of fashion and a fine female, up to every rig and row in town, and only a fool would hurt—but I hadn't known Susan then, and, well, I want to ask you: Can you see Audrey following the drum?"

"If you mean can I see Audrey as the wife of a military man in active service, frankly, no. Good God, no!" Lord Merlin laughed at the very idea. "What an entourage she would bring to camp! Can you see Audrey washing her own laundry and making bivouac?"

"No, exactly not! Told me once she'd never even been in the kitchens of her own house! Besides, I don't think m'mother would like it above half! That is, I'm the head of the family now! Got to think about m'mother and my sisters. They like Audrey well enough, I suppose, but as m'wife? Also, there's the matter of money! I'm a fairly comfortable man, but Audrey's as rich as a golden ball! A man don't like to feel that he's a fortune hunter! Which I am not! No need! M'mother and sisters dote on Susan, though! And so do I! She'll follow the drum readily enough!"

"Yes, I think I can see that."

"You can?"

Lord Merlin was beginning to feel a trifle bored with this excess of feelings. "Of course I can. So, all you need to do is offer for her. I assume Miss Dysart's feelings for you are fixed?"

"It's not that simple, as well you know!"

"Audrey, at bottom, has a great deal of sense. She will see immediately how it is."

"The thing of it is, I've been offering for Audrey all along!"

"Has she accepted?"

"No," the major said. "But—"

"You think she may be offended and feel that you have been courting another behind her back, so to speak."

"Not only that, and I'll admit that's a problem, anywise you look at it, but Audrey's got it into her mind that you and Susan might still make a match of it. Susan don't like you above half."

Lord Merlin laughed. "Nor can I blame her! I seem to have done everything within my power to frighten her, it would seem! And, Audrey—Audrey is a managing person who is far too used to having her own way. It's time she learned there are consequences to attempting to run everyone else's lives for them."

"That's another thing. Don't think I wouldn't be living under the cat's paw with her, because I know I would, if she did say yes, which she could, still! Look at what happened to Old Hook! Met Miss Pakenham, showed an interest, went off to war for twelve years, he never writes, she never writes, no communication whatsoever! He comes home and she expects him to marry her! And he does! Expected to! Damned unhappy situation for all concerned!"

"I see your point. But you must recall, Audrey has said time and time again she don't wish to be married!" Merlin said thoughtfully. "A suitable match for Audrey would have to be a strong man indeed, to make her change her mind."

"And that ain't me! I am in love with Susan, and she is in love with me. She'd marry me, if she didn't think it would set Audrey off. She feels grateful to Audrey for all she's done! Doesn't want to hurt her! And neither do I."

"No, I think not."

"There's nothing to be done but blow my brains out," the major sighed.

"If that's the way you're going to handle this, then you deserve neither lady!" Merlin advised him. "But I think I may have a plan, if you are willing to listen. I think we both may find that we will attain that which we most desire. But it will take a little patience."

The major grasped his hands. "I will wait any length of time, I will listen to anything, if only Susan and I may be married. I can say that neither she nor I will lack for courage!"

"The first thing I will ask you to do is let go of my hands! This rain is foul enough without having to handle the reins over your sticky-fingered grip!" Lord Merlin said testily. "Young love! Good God, spare me!"

Happily oblivious to this conversation, over the next few days, Lady Wellford threw herself wholeheartedly into designs for the ball. As soon as Mrs. Shelby was fully recovered, Audrey enlisted her aid in venturing to Merlin House to see what was to be seen.

"Having coped for eleven years as a widow, I am sure that planning a ball will present no hardship," she said to Mrs. Shelby. "After all, there are two of us, and two females are more than equal to one man when it comes to putting on an entertainment. I have planned a few balls in my time, you know."

Mrs. Shelby, however, still looked doubtful. "It somehow seems encroaching to just march into Lord Merlin's house and take over in this fashion," she said.

"You need not worry! Merlin has given us carte blanche to do as we please," Audrey said briskly.

Following on his lordship's last visit to Half Moon Street, they met to discuss the arrangements for the coming out. Audrey, very smart in a cardinal driving coat and black grosgrain toque, deposited Susan at Grosvenor Square with the Shelby sisters, and took up Mrs. Shelby, who was attired in a very becoming blue pelisse and Parisian bonnet. The two ladies proceeded to Merlin House to survey the raw clay from which they hoped to mold a most spectacular coming-out ball.

"I am so glad that I can rely upon Giles to keep Susan entertained," Audrey said. "I understand he is taking the girls to the Green Park this afternoon to see the balloon ascension!"

"Oh, yes! Emily and Jane are both looking forward to it. Imagine soaring up that high!" Mrs. Shelby shuddered.

"There was a fire balloon at Vauxhall Gardens about ten years ago. I saw that, and I said 'no more!'" Audrey agreed.

It had been a number of years since she had been inside Merlin House, and as she brought her phaeton to a halt before its Georgian portals, she sighed.

"I heard that before old Lord Merlin got so queer, he was a great one to entertain," Audrey said. "Oh, they say the balls he had here when his wife was still alive were magnificent! She died in childbirth, you know, and it was very sad! I remember, right after Wellford and I were married, he held a small dinner party, and I was quite in awe! As Madam Hart would say, we could not ask for a better stage!"

Lord Merlin's steward, as he had predicted, was as anxious as the ladies to launch a lavish entertainment upon Society. Monsieur Levec, a shrewd French émigré who had ordered a very grand ducal household before the Revolution, recognized quality when he saw it, and quickly led the ladies through the grand hallway into the ballroom that occupied nearly all of the second floor of one wing. It was a long, narrow room with high ceilings and the highly decorative plaster panels so common in the last century. It was also enormous, empty, and echoing with the revenants of long-forgotten dancers. The faint, ghostly smell of roses and dust hung in the still, closed air. "We can accommodate five hundred without creating a sad squeeze," Monsieur said proudly.

Gesturing to a footman to remove a holland cover from a fragile crystal chandelier, drawing back a dusty drape from a window to reveal the garden below, using his own handkerchief to dust a spindly ballroom chair, he entered into all of their plans with the greatest enthusiasm.

"You do not know how long I have waited for just such an event as this!" he said with the true fervor of the artist. "When I was with the Duc des Foailles, there were balls every night! Such magnificent dinners as we had! Twenty courses, and each one in pastry, baked in the shape of a different animal! We started *avec les oiseux,* vegetable pastries in the shape of little birds, and ended with *le sorbet glacé,* the whole in the shape of *Madame la Reine* of gracious memory, although of course at the time, we did not appreciate her as we should have!" Monsieur Levec waxed nostalgic, dabbing at his eyes with his handkerchief. "*Pours les jeunes mademoiselles,* we can do no less! *L'ancien régime* may be dead, *mais l'esprit* lives on!" He clasped his hands together in inspiration. "*L'heure bleue!* That shall be our *thème!*"

Lady Wellford and Mrs. Shelby, who between the two of them possessed schoolroom French that was, at best, limited, smiled and nodded, borne away on the tide of Monsieur Levec's enthusiasm. "I read the Society news, and I see that all the ladies decorate their ballrooms with pink silk tents. Pah! *C'est l'ennui! Non, mesdames! Il faut avoir l'heure bleue!*"

Audrey was beginning to think she understood what had impelled Lord Merlin to find pressing business in the country. It was hard to picture him going into raptures over a ballroom from the *ancien régime,* let alone the theme of the blue hour, that deliciate time of day between twilight and dusk, if she remembered correctly.

"Blue! We shall drape the ballroom in blue silk— with spangled stars! It will appear as a starry night, only imagine!" Monsieur Levec said, pacing about the vast and empty room, waving a hand as if it were a magic wand. And indeed, beneath the weight of his considerable enthusiasm, Audrey and Mrs. Shelby could almost see that blue silk, celestial blue, and those glittering, silver-spangled stars transforming this hollow, echoing room, silent so long, filled only with ghosts, into a magical place.

"And flowers there must be, all white and yellow,

and tied with gold and silver ribbons!

"I read *dans les journaux de société* that the grand ladies all have the Pandean Pipes or the Scots Band! *Encore, c'est l'ennui.* For the music, we must have someone different, some orchestra that is more exciting! And we must have the waltz!"

"At a private ball, Monsieur Levec?" Mrs. Shelby asked doubtfully.

"*Mais oui, Madame.*" He gave a Gallic shrug. "It is my understanding that the waltz is danced everywhere in Paris."

That must be enough to settle it for them. If the waltz was danced in Paris, then they must have an orchestra that played waltzes.

"I personally shall scour the city for the right musicans," Monsieur Levec promised. "These floors shall shine! The chandeliers will be taken down and scrubbed so that they sparkle! The light of a thousand candles shall reflect the jewels of the ladies present! The orchestra will play the waltz, people will dance! It will be a night to remember!" He sighed in rapture.

He clapped his hands and the footmen disappeared. "Now, ladies, if you will step into the library, we shall discuss the refreshments!"

Audrey, so used to managing, found the experience of being gently but ruthlessly managed herself quite novel. Cast about as she might for some spoke of her own to thrust into Monsieur Levec's plans, she could find nothing that she could possibly add or even protest.

"You must pardon me for saying so, *mesdames,* but as admirable as the new Lord Merlin is as an employer, his style is not one that has so far led to *les grandes entertainments* so worthy of this noble family!

A female touch is required, *non?* All of my training has been for *les grandes hôtels*—the great establishments of my country! *Monsieur le vicomte* has not fully employed my skills, which are considerable. *Pour moi,* this is a dream come true! Have no fear, I shall take care of all details. You ladies have only to state your preferences and it shall be done!"

"And they say it's hard to get good help these days," Mrs. Shelby whispered to Audrey as Monsieur Levec went to hurry the footmen along.

In a moment he had returned with a sheaf of menus and a dazzling variety of wines from Merlin's cellars. "My lord wishes you to choose those which you would like to have served. We have some very fine claret and amontillado laid down in the old lord's time, and also, may I recommend you sample the oh-three hock and the ninety-eight sauternes? Alas, the sherry was smuggled during the war, and is not up to snuff, but the champagne is quite potable."

"Oh, but we can't possibly take up the wines from Lord Merlin's cellar!" Audrey exclaimed. "We shall of course order them from Gunter's, together with the food and flowers."

Monsieur Levec's look was horrified. "*Mais,* milady, Lord Merlin left specific instruction that you are to draw from the resources of the house."

"We can't do that! That would be *excessively* encroaching!" Mrs. Shelby exclaimed. "It is good enough of Lord Merlin to allow us to use his house. We cannot exhaust his cellars also!"

Monsieur Levec bowed. "I have my orders, madam," he said firmly. "Milord was most specific that Merlin House would provide all that you need *pour le bal. Il dit* 'All or nothing, tell Lady Wellford.'" Monsieur's little mustaches quivered. "Milord says, 'The ladies shall not trifle their heads over expenses. When I give *carte blanche,* I give *carte blanche.*'" He spread his hands. "It is not wise to offend milord," he added.

"So I've discovered," Audrey said drily.

"But Lady Wellford, we can hardly ask Lord Merlin to pay for the ball!" Mrs. Shelby said in great anxiety.

"I can see he means this to be a tease to me! Perhaps he means to use this to discourage us from using his ballroom," Audrey said. "Very well, if that is the way he wants to play this game, then he wins this hand." *But not the game,* she thought. She smiled up at Monsieur Levec. "Monsieur, it must be as Lord Merlin wishes."

Levec's relief was obvious. Once again, he beamed. "Then mesdames will allow me to pour the wines? You will of course wish to sample the vintages."

"We need Sir Peyton for this," Audrey remarked lightly to Mrs. Shelby, who still looked doubtful. "Don't worry," she added in an undertone. "When he receives all the bills and has a fine tantrum, I shall write a draft on my bank for him. This is Merlin's idea of humor, I fear."

"Oh, dear, do you think you should?" Mrs. Shelby asked.

Audrey patted her hand. "Trust me!" she replied. "I shall not involve you in this, I promise!"

With that assurance, Mrs. Shelby had to be content. If these were the games played by the fashionable fribbles of London, she was beginning to feel that she was very much better off in West Country circles.

However, the ladies tasted the various wines that were set before them and pronounced them more than adequate for the supper, and by the time they had

had one delicate sip of each of the various vintages presented for their approval, they were much more in charity with the absent viscount.

Levec made a note of those that were acceptable, and several times made tactful suggestions of his own.

Again, Audrey was left with the distinct feeling that she was being more managed than managing, although this was done so skillfully she could find no way to protest without seeming boorish.

"I always say," he murmured, scribbling furiously in his wine book, "that one should chose the wines and then the food. Now, if you ladies will wait, I shall summon the chef."

"Oh, no! We must have the food catered!" Mrs. Shelby protested. "To put the staff out any further would be wrong!"

But the viscount's chef, another Gallic professional, was summoned from the kitchens, and, with a sheaf of menus carried by a minion almost as toplofty as himself, proceeded to shower the ladies with suggestions as to what to serve for the dinner and the refreshments.

Since this artist had worked in the kitchens of the most noted gastronome in Paris before the Revolution, he, too, had his ideas about what was edible.

"*En l'Angleterre,* c'est le *pomme de terre, toujours le* boiled *pomme de terre,*" he said, shaking his head at this foolishness. "It comes in with the soup, it is served with the fish, with the meat, with a fowl and with the dessert, in all the homes of the English. For this ball, for this supper, there will be *no* boiled *pommes de terre!*" he declared with such great passion that even Audrey was intimidated.

"Heavens! What will people eat?" Mrs. Shelby asked.

To answer her question, the chef began to display samples of his gustatory masterpieces so mouth-watering that even Audrey had to sample at least two of everything.

There were tiny squabs wrapped in delicate pastry, lightly seasoned with tarragon. There were ham and cheese tarts baked in thick cream; there were sautéed endive savories, caviar bisques, green peppercorn pâtés, infinitesimal loaves of perfect bread stuffed with spiced beef. There were vol-au-vents with all manner of wonderful fillings involving fowl or fish and heavenly sauces. There were smoked oysters, and sole in a light-as-air butter and truffle dressing. And the desserts! *Chocolat à la duchesse, bombe richelieu, petites gateaux,* strawberry trifles, and crème glacé.

"I think seven courses with five or six removes for each course will do very well," Monsieur Levec said, writing down the ladies' choices in his little book. "You need only leave it all to me, and it shall be done!" he promised. "All you need to do is send out your invitation cards and wear your prettiest gowns. It will be a night that all London will remember."

As they drove away, Mrs. Shelby sighed. "No wonder Lord Merlin went into the country! If my staff fed and wined me like that, I'd be as drunk as a lord and as big as a barrow!"

9

There was not a morning that went by
when the door knocker was silent, an afternoon left
unfilled with engagements for luncheons, picnics, and
parades, nor an evening when Lady Wellford and
her niece were not out upon the town, attending a
rout, an illumination, a concert, an opera, or a ball.
The Season was in full swing, the marriage mart open
for business, and Susan Dysart was proving to have
attracted more than her fair share of suitors.

Young men in uniform, young men down from
Oxford, young dandies in painfully stylish waistcoats,
young bucks aspiring to the Four Horse Club, young
Corinthians who yearned after sport, pious young
men who would take orders, brilliant young men
who would stand for Parliament, rich young men who
had Expectations, poor young men who had Hopes,

all of them seemed to find a second home in Lady Wellford's drawing room, where they lounged about on the furniture, availed themselves of the offerings from Audrey's cellars and kitchens, turning the pages while Susan played the pianoforte and singing along with the current ballads of the day. Some of them composed poetry, which they read aloud. Or they played cards, or they begged Susan to ride with them in the park or grant them a dance at that night's ball. More and more bouquets of flowers blossomed into the drawing room with every passing day. Some of them developed little *tendres* for Audrey, which she found quite touching, but she gently and firmly depressed their hopes. Nonetheless, she received her fair share of poetry and flowers and invitations to dance with young and callow men who gazed at her as if she were a goddess.

Major Shelby, claiming the press of obligations at his mess, had suddenly become very scarce, which slightly annoyed Lady Wellford. "Just when I am in need of an escort, you desert me, too?" she exclaimed. The major grabbed his hat and ran, which annoyed her even more. Really, she thought, it was time to examine his conduct—when she had the time.

Audrey was delighted by Susan's success. She saw it as a great credit to her work. "I think she has taken very well," she told Miss Fishbank. "Now, if she would just choose one of these young men, we could have the ball, announce the engagement, and have done with the whole thing. I am quite given up on Merlin coming up to scratch. I think he will die a bachelor!"

However, she was discovering that being the chaperone of a popular girl had its drawbacks. Susan only had to mention that she liked pineapples to have the entire city's supply nearly bought out within a day.

The chef was in despair. "What am I do with all these pineapples?" he wailed.

Otterbine grew weary and spoke of retirement to that little public house he had so long dreamed of opening. Wescott grew pettish when Susan thoughtlessly borrowed Audrey's fripperies. She and Susan had words. Susan sulked when Audrey overruled her. Audrey, unused to adolescent moods, grew exasperated. There were tears, and things were smoothed over before that night's ball.

"The truth is," Audrey confided to Miss Fishbank, "It's exhausting, all this gadding about and all of these young people hanging about! It would be perfectly all right with me, if only I didn't *always* have to be there, feeling like a militia man, keeping everyone in order! It's dreary! Susan is well enough, but I *am* tired. This debutante business is tiresome, always having to chaperone, never having any time for oneself or one's friends. What I wouldn't give for an entertaining evening with some grown-ups! Real conversation about politics and books and thoughts! Something other than beaux and balls! If not for you, dear Appie, I think I would go mad!"

They were working on a list of invitations for the ball. That is to say, Audrey was making up a list, and Miss Fishbank was writing them out in her fine copperplate hand.

Blessed peace had descended upon the household, temporarily, at least, Miss Dysart, Miss Shelby, and Miss Jane being engaged in an expedition to view a mock naval battle at Regent's Park, chaperoned by Mrs. Shelby. Audrey had presumed their host of suitors had gone in the same direction, only to find one of

them still in the drawing room. Since it was not Miss
Dysart, Miss Shelby, or Miss Jane who had engaged
his fancy, but the dashing Lady Wellford, Audrey
had been forced to listen to young Lord Tilghman
practice his nineteen-year-old seductive wiles on her.
It was a quarter hour before she was able to send him
off with a flea in his ear, sadder but wiser. A lady of
fashion who was a decade older than himself was
well up to snuff on the manners of far more hardened
flirts than he. Still, it had been an unpleasant episode,
more awkward than painful, and it had put Audrey's
temper, already frayed, on the edge, so much so that
she had turned the biting edge of her wit on him.

"Was I too hard in him?" she wondered.

"No," she answered herself. "If he had been
amusing about it, he would have done better. Perhaps
this way he'll learn a lesson."

Still, the idea that she should even have to tolerate
such lèse-majesté profoundly offended her sense of
self-importance, and that must *never* happen!

"At least not with some green sprig!" she muttered,
ruthlessly crossing his name off the ball list and
consigning him to social oblivion.

"Very correct!" Miss Fishbank said. "I never did
like his mother, either! A most encroaching female!"
She punctuated this comment with a cough.

"Oh, Appie!" Audrey exclaimed. "You can't be
getting sick, can you? Let me feel your forehead, my
dear!" She rose from the table and pressed her hand
against Miss Fishbank's forehead. "Appie, you are
burning up! How long have you felt like this?"

"Well, I had a little tickle in my throat last night,
but I felt a little more the thing this morning." She
coughed again. "But after lunch, I just felt a trifle

feverish. Of course, I'll be all right in a moment. And all these invitations must be addressed—"

"This to the invitations!" Audrey snapped her fingers. "I do believe you've caught that stupid influenza from the Shelbys! Appie, you come upstairs right now and crawl into bed! I'll send a footman over to Harley Street for Dr. Bayley."

"Oh, I am certain there is no need for the doctor to be summoned . . ." Miss Fishbank said. She gripped the arms of her chair until her knuckles were white. Her arms shook as she tried unsuccessfully to rise.

"Appie, how could I not see how pale you are?" Audrey asked, supporting her former governess. "Let me summon Otterbine! He'll help us get upstairs."

In a very short while, Miss Fishbank was in her bed, and Dr. Bayley, summoned from Harley Street, was completing his examination.

"Well, ma'am," he said, "you've contracted the influenza, there's no doubt about that. And a good thing Lady Wellford called me in early, for I am here to tell you that you must hang up your dancing shoes for at least a week!"

Miss Fishbank smiled feebly. "Oh, Doctor!" she sighed. Like many women, she drew confidence from his jovial manner.

"I shall call again tomorrow to see how you do, but for the time being, it should be bed rest, alcohol baths, broth and barley water for you, ma'am."

One of the maids was called to sit by her, while Lady Wellford and the doctor had a private conference in the hall outside her bedroom. "It's been going around," he said, shaking his head. "Probably as a result of all the strangers in town. Miss Fishbank is a good patient, but I should hate to see her overtax

herself by getting up too early! At her age, it's wisest
to keep her quiet and let her sleep. If she becomes
feverish, you may give her three grains of laudanum
in a glass of wine. I expect it will run its course in a
week."

"Just as long as she's all right," Audrey said anx-
iously. "I will do anything you say!"

Dr. Bayley peered at her over his spectacles.
"You're looking a bit peaked yourself, Lady Wellford.
I would hold rope, if I were you!"

Audrey shook her head. "Nonsense, Doctor! I am
never unwell!" she said firmly.

She spent the rest of the afternoon watching over
Miss Fishbank.

"If you would just bring those invitations up
here together with my lap board, I am sure I could
have them done," Miss Fishbank said fretfully, picking at the covers. "They really should go out, you
know."

"They can be sent out to a calligrapher," Audrey
said firmly. "The thing is not to worry about them
yourself! I want you well and back on your feet, my
dear Appie! You know there is no need to worry
yourself over trivialities!"

Still, Miss Fishbank fretted, turning restlessly in
her bed and worrying about all the things being left
undone that needed her attention. "Tonight's menu?
Who will look at the menu? Is anyone making sure
that the housemaids are dusting the breakfast parlor?"
she asked plaintively.

Audrey gently adjusted her cap and dabbed
hartshorn water on her temples. "Now, Appie, you
know that's not important! I don't care what we have
for dinner!"

"But Susan! I promised Susan that I would chaperone her and the girls to Vauxhall Gardens tonight! It was to be my little treat for them. . . ." She tried to sit up in bed, and it was all that Audrey could do to keep her down.

Looking about for something to distract her, Audrey's eye landed on a stack of books on the table. "Jane Austen!" she murmured to herself. "Thank the Lord for Miss Austen!"

Miss Fishbank being a great admirer of the works of Miss Austen, Audrey was able to keep her still and occupied by reading aloud from the first volume of *Emma*, which had just been published. It distracted them both, and kept Audrey reading long after Miss Fishbank had fallen into a fatigued and unquiet slumber.

Audrey was sitting by the coal fire, reading, when Susan, still in her pelisse and bonnet, knocked on the door.

"Is Miss Fishbank not well?" she asked.

Audrey held a finger to her lips. "Influenza," she said.

Susan nodded. "Is there anything that I can do?" she asked.

Audrey shook her head. "No, she's to have bed rest and barley water. If you like, you may change for dinner, and afterwards, we will write out those invitations."

"Vauxhall Gardens!" Miss Fishbank cried, sitting bolt upright. Her face was flushed, her eyes glittered, and her jaw was quivering. "I promised the girls that they would go to Vauxhall tonight!" She groped on the nightstand for her spectacles. "I must get up!"

Susan rushed to console her. "We can always go

another time, Miss Fishbank!" she said, taking the older woman's hand. "It's really not important! The important thing is that you rest! You are very ill, ma'am!"

"Never let it be said that Appolonia Fishbank broke a promise! My father, the rector, would be horrified!" Miss Fishbank was greatly agitated and feverish, it was clear.

"Now, Appie," Audrey said, but Miss Fishbank was having none of it. "I must get up and get dressed! Where is my good brown velvet dress?"

"Please, Miss Fishbank," Susan pleaded. "Calm yourself!"

"It's the fever," Audrey said. "She doesn't know what she's saying."

"Indeed I do!" Miss Fishbank replied indignantly. "Don't think I don't know what's what, because I do! Now, Audrey, let me out of this bed!"

In the end, there was nothing to be done but that Audrey must promise that she would take on the party at Vauxhall Gardens. It was the only way either of them could find that would make the older woman lie down and rest. As soon as she was reassured that Audrey would act as her deputy, she relaxed a great deal and even agreed to a few drops of laudanum in a glass of mulled wine.

"And don't think I won't be watching to make sure you go, because I will, Audrey! You're not too old to break a promise, young lady!" she said sharply. "I can always go live with my sister in Bath!"

"Well," Audrey sighed. "I guess there's nothing for it! When Appie talks about living with her sister in Bath, I must listen." She stroked the older woman's forehead. "I shall do as you wish, my dear."

Miss Fishbank leaned back against the pillows and closed her eyes, satisfied. "It shall never be said that Appolonia Fishbank broke her promise!"

She promptly fell into a deep and drugged sleep.

As a young bride, Audrey had thought Vauxhall Gardens one of the most exciting places in London. In addition to the landscaped grounds, which dated back to the Restoration, the Gardens boasted spectacular fire and waterworks displays, musical entertainments, balloon ascensions, acrobats, firewalkers and high-wire artists. Themes were changed often; in this season of victory, there was a reenactment of a sea battle with cannon fire and lifelike men o' war, all set to music and billed as The Naumachia. There were booths where the entertainment could be seen while a party consumed a stingily provisioned supper for a guinea and drank strong punch priced at seven shillings the glass. The attraction that drew Londoners high and low and gave the Gardens their slightly raffish reputation were the various walks. These were promenades winding through the trees and gardens where a rendezvous could be arranged or an encounter effected with a stranger. Audrey knew them as well as any other lady of fashion, and for this reason she was determined that the girls in her charge would be allowed to stray within a mile of these paths over the last breath from her dying body.

Already feeling burdened by worry over Miss Fishbank's condition, she was hardly in the mood to escort three giggling, lively young women to a public place. She sent a note around to the Albany, demanding that Major Shelby accompany her, if only to keep order. The footman reported that the major was not at home, and the note had been left with his subaltern, who promised that he should have it the minute he returned, but by the time the Shelby sisters arrived on her doorstep, there was still no reply.

But Susan was enthusiastic, and Emily and Jane, excited by the prospect of an evening supported by the worldly and glamorous Lady Wellford, rather than the staid and decorous Miss Fishbank, were equally animated.

Taking a supper box on the Grove, where the concerts played, Audrey was immediately annoyed by the ogling and bold remarks of a party of young men seated in an adjoining box. They were decidedly of vulgar origins, apprentices or clerks out on the town, and as such, exactly the sort of forbidden fruit that genteel young girls would be interested in—at a safe distance. What they were too young and too naive to comprehend was that there was no safe distance at Vauxhall Gardens.

"There's a bevy of beauties!" one of them said, leaning from his box almost into theirs. "How are you ladies doin' tonight? Want some company?"

"I'll thank you to mind your manners!" Audrey said indignantly. This response, which should have depressed their pretensions immediately, was greeted with snickers.

Audrey felt the want of a male in their company immediately, and wished that she had not told her footman to wait with the barouche.

One young girl Audrey might have been able to keep strictly under control, but a covey of three excited maidens was beyond her capacity to do more than snap "Behave, do!" from time to time. The addition of a bowl of Vauxhall punch, served with their dinner, did little to suppress their high spirits. At first, they kept their eyes downcast, pretending to ignore the interested young men, then gradually began to glance at them, then finally, emboldened perhaps by the punch, began to flirt whenever Audrey's attention was engaged elsewhere.

"It's just a flirtation," Miss Jane simpered. Susan and Emily giggled.

The result was that the giggling girls calmed down for as much as five minutes before bursting out again in peals of laughter when one of the young men in the adjoining box said or did something to attract their attention.

When Audrey overheard Miss Jane attempting to whisper to one of the young men behind her back, she tossed her napkin down. Her head ached and she was bone tired. "That's enough!" she snapped. "Now, we're going home!"

Three astonished pairs of eyes stared at her as if she had suddenly and magically transformed herself into an ogress before their very eyes. Susan's lower lip trembled and her eyes grew watery.

"Oh, Aunt!" she breathed. "How could you be so Gothic?"

"Hellfire and brimstone!" Audrey exclaimed. She signaled the waiter and threw some pound notes on the table.

One of the young men whistled.

"And in front of my friends, too!" Susan added.

"There's an abbess and her high flyers! Stay, sweet beauties, and let your keeper go!"

Another one of the boys booed loudly.

The girls, realizing the game had gone too far, flushed to the roots of their hair and gathered up their things, frightened and silent as Audrey, majestically shaking out her skirts, herded them away from the Gardens and toward the waiting carriage.

It was not until she had left the Shelby sisters at their door that she turned the full extent of her wrath upon Susan.

"I have never witnessed such bad behavior in my life! If you wish to conduct a flirtation with every vulgarian on the town, then perhaps you should go back to Bleakfriars!" she stormed. Her head throbbed, she was out of temper and barely knew what she was saying, except that she was much too angry to deal with her niece at that moment.

Susan cowered in a corner of the barouche, and then when they came to the front door of Half Moon Street, fled up the stairs in tears.

Audrey listened to the door to Susan's room slam, then wearily made her way to Miss Fishbank's room, where she found her former governess still fitfully sleeping.

"Is that you, Audrey?" she asked weakly, as Audrey bent over the bed, peering down at her by the low light of a lamp.

"I'm here," Audrey said, stroking Miss Fishbank's forehead. She was still feverish; her eyes, beneath half closed lids, glittered. The hand that reached out for Audrey's was cold and weak.

"Good." Miss Fishbank's eyes closed again.

"Miss's been sleepin', on and off, and she woke up a while ago and drank some barley water," the little maid told her. "I been bathin' her head with hartshorn water like you said, my lady."

Audrey thanked her. "I'll change my clothes and sit with her now," she said.

Wescott changed her into a robe dress and massaged her temples. "You sit with her for a while, my lady, and I'll come in and spell you. You looked fagged to death yourself," the abigail said.

"No, I'm perfectly all right. Just tired to death, that's all, and this headache is plaguing me."

It was midnight when Audrey settled down in Miss Fishbank's room. The governess was sleeping still, tossing a bit less restlessly now. When she saw Audrey, she muttered something, and settled back into slumber.

Audrey opened *Emma* again, and by the dim light of the lamp, began to read. But even Miss Austen's astute prose failed to keep her awake.

When Wescott came in an hour or so later, she found both ladies slumbering peacefully. She looked about, and satisfied that all was well, went back to Miss Fishbank's dressing room, where a trundle bed had been set up within earshot.

It was not long before she, too, was asleep.

In the morning, Miss Fishbank declared herself to feel much better. She was able to sit up in bed, propped up by pillows, to eat a little toast dipped in tea. "I feel a little weak," Miss Fishbank admitted. But she was still far from well.

Audrey was relieved to see her feeling more the thing, and left her reading the Court Circular while she went in search of Susan.

"I was hard on her last night, and I need to smooth things down," she told her erstwhile governess.

But when she knocked on Susan's door, there was no answer. "Susan, please let me in," she pleaded, only to be greeted by silence. "I need to talk to you."

Still, silence.

Audrey tried the door. The knob turned in her hand, and she opened it.

The first thing she noticed was that the bed was undisturbed. The pink coverlet was smooth, and the curtains were still drawn.

Then she noted the eerie stillness and order of the room, as if it had long been unoccupied.

And then she saw the note propped up on the dressing table.

Audrey's heart leaped as she snatched it up.

Dear Aunt Audrey
 There is no way I can ever face you again after last night's Display. I have betrayed you at Every Turn. I colde not stay and allow you to nuture a Viper in your Bosom, becuase Major Shelby loves me and I love him and we have gone away to be married becuase I can not bear to go back To Bleakfriars. Pleese do not try to Stop Us.
 We will live our happines Forever Over-shadoed knowing how much we have hurt you. I am very sorry.
                        Your Retshed Niece
                           Susan Dysart
P.S. Don't Blame Jane and Emily. I put them up to it last night.

The pathos of this missive was lost in the moment as Audrey struggled to decipher Susan's ornate handwriting and erratic spelling. That the paper was liberally blotted with teardrops did little to help.

"Hellfire and brimstone!" Audrey exclaimed when

she finally unraveled the message. "So that's the lay of the land! Susan and Giles! How could I have been so foolish as not to see—but they are perfect for each other!" She started to laugh, very much amused. Then a dark thought struck her. "Elopement! Oh, no! Not when I've put so much work into that ball, you two don't!"

Elopement was out of the question. It would leave a scandal that would forever tarnish Susan's name and jeopardize Giles's chances of advancement in the army. They were doubtless even now on their way to Gretna Green, and they must be stopped!

"Wescott!" she called, striding toward her room. "Lay out my brown bombazine driving habit and tell Otterbine to send to the stables for my phaeton!"

Miss Fishbank peered out of her room. Her face was still as pale as her cap. "My dear Audrey, whatever is the matter?" she asked.

Audrey handed her the note. "Read this! That silly girl has eloped! With Giles of all people! I must write a note immediately to Mrs. Shelby! There seems to have been a plot afoot."

"My dear, no need to let the whole house know!" Miss Fishbank admonished her. She peered nearsightedly down at the note. "Dear me, whatever next?" she murmured.

"Why not? They'll all know soon enough!" Audrey retorted. "Good God! What madness! Appie, go back to bed! I'll handle this!"

Fifteen minutes later, she came down the stairs in her riding habit, pulling on her driving gloves.

Just as she was walking out the door, she heard a familiar voice hailing her and she turned to see Lord Merlin just descending from his curricle.

"I have never been so glad to see anyone in my life!" Audrey exclaimed. "Quick, you've got to come with me!"

Merlin raised an eyebrow. "Bit early to be riding in the park," he drawled.

Audrey shook her head. "Oh, I am at the end of my rope! Susan has eloped with Giles!" She tugged at the sleeve of his jacket. "You must come with me, Merlin, and bring them back! I'm sure they have gone to Gretna Green! They can't have gotten a great start!"

Merlin raised an eyebrow, but did not immediately move.

Audrey tugged again. "Nicholas, I need you! I can't do this alone! Come with me, I'm pleading with you! That pair of ninnies shall become properly engaged and it will be announced at the ball! One scandalous female in the Dysart family is enough!"

"Well!" Merlin tilted back his shallow crowned beaver hat. "Since you plead, Audrey, how can I resist? Were you planning to fetch them back in that two-seater phaeton of yours? Where shall you put your groom and Major Shelby?"

By now, Audrey was on the verge of hysterics. "I don't know! I don't care! We must find them and bring them back before it is too late!"

"Then let us go!" Merlin said. "But this time, we'll take my curricle! I have the greatest horror of being cramped into a phaeton with a weeping girl and a sulky boy!"

He swept Audrey up into his curricle. After a brief conference with his groom, he joined her. "I've sent my man on to get a saddle horse. Perhaps if he rides ahead, he can find them, or at the very least trace their steps. One man on horseback is faster, you know. Don't worry, Audrey, between the two of us, I think we can put a stop to this."

He spoke with so much confidence that she allowed herself some hope. Perhaps, after all, there would be a happy ending. Just having someone to share the burden with was a relief. She held on to her hat as he started down the street at a spanking pace, threading his way though the morning traffic with impressive skill.

Audrey relaxed just a little. Her headache, which had been dully throbbing since she had awakened, began to recede a little.

"I imagine you find all of this very amusing," she said as Merlin threaded his team out of the city. Under other circumstances, she could see where she would have enjoyed this jaunt. He had a fine team of bays, and the day was pleasant, although a few clouds lingered at the edges of the horizon, above the church steeples and the rooftops of the city.

"Not at all! I am only sorry for you to lose your swain in such a way."

"My swain?" Audrey looked at him incredulously. "Oh, you mean Giles! It was never serious, you know. At least on my part! In fact, I think that he and Susan are well matched. I felt sorry for you, for losing my niece!"

"But I never even wanted her, something you seem to have a great deal of trouble getting through that lovely head of yours," Merlin remarked matter-of-factly.

"Yes," Audrey said. "I think that I did, and I was wrong about that."

"Hold! Do I hear Lady Wellford admitting that she might have made an error?"

In spite of herself, Audrey laughed. "You may have. Oh, Merlin, I hate to admit it, but I very well might be in error once—but only once, of course—in a great while!"

He threw back his head and roared, very nearly colliding with a cart of cabbages. Regaining himself quickly, he slid his team expertly between the cart and the oncoming Great Northern mail coach. With inches to spare on either side, he brought them around safely.

"Neat to the inch!" Audrey said admiringly.

"You shouldn't make me laugh," he said in mock reproval. "It's very bad form to distract a Nonpareil when he's driving a fresh team!"

"Teams! Merlin, do you have any money?" A horrible thought had just struck Audrey. "I came away without a shilling or a change of clothes! And it will take money to stop at posting houses and change teams!" She clutched at his sleeve.

"We can stop at Merlinford. It's only a few miles out of the way. They will see to everything we need, and we may be on our way. Once we are out of city traffic, we will make better time," Merlin replied easily. He squeezed her hand reassuringly. "Don't worry, Audrey! We can do this, you know!"

"Oh, I hope so! Let me know when you wish me to take the reins, will you?"

"Never fear."

How it came about that she felt her eyes growing heavier and a great fatigue overtaking her, she did not know. But once they had passed Finchley Common, she leaned against Merlin's broad shoulder and fell into a catnap. The sun was warm, and his driving coat, with its many capes, was soft and inviting.

It was only when she started to cough that she awakened with a start. Cold droplets of rain were splashing down on them, and Merlin had wrapped her inside his coat. It was not an entirely unpleasant feeling. "Where are we?" she asked, sitting bolt upright and trying to shed herself of his coat. Fine rain splashed into her face. It soaked her clothes, ran down into her hair, ruined the feathers on her hat. She shivered with ague.

"Almost to Merlinford," the viscount replied. "Two more miles."

"Good."

Audrey coughed again. Her throat itched, and her eyes were running, and she ached all over. Every time the curricle wheels hit a rut, it was as if she had been struck. Since she was never sick, she felt annoyed with herself for betraying so much weakness. She felt in her pocket for a handkerchief, and came up empty-handed. "Hellfire and brimstone," she said weakly.

"Use mine. Audrey, are you sure you feel well? You don't look at all the thing, my girl."

"I'm not your girl, and I'm perfectly fine," she said, but she coughed into his large linen kerchief anyway. "I'm sorry I'm so out of sorts, but consider the circumstances!"

She looked about them, but all she could see was fog and rain and gray fields that rolled away into the mist. They must have been traveling for two or three hours while she was asleep, she thought.

He opened his coat and pulled her back into the sheltering warmth of the heavy wool. She leaned against him, too exhausted to resist, and when he wrapped his arm around her, she snuggled into the comfort of his broad chest.

From a great distance away, she could hear him humming softly, snatches of an old ballad. It was like a dream. She wished she could go back to sleep, but her head throbbed so that she could barely think. She fell into a fit of dry coughing again.

It seemed forever before the curricle stopped, and she had only a dreamer's impression of strong hands guiding her down from the trap, of distant voices that were yet so close talking urgently.

"I am never ill," she said. "This is very silly. We must go on immediately." The rain was falling very fast now, and the fog was growing thicker. She was dimly aware of a set of gray stone steps and the ornately carved lintel of a massive old door.

"Merlin, they will be in Gretna Green if we don't hurry!" she pleaded, clutching at his sleeve. But when she reached out for his sleeve, she clutched only air.

She thought she was falling. but strong hands caught her and she was lifted up, light as air.

What happened after that, she was not entirely certain.

She was aware that she was not well, and that she was dreaming dreams that were neither awakening nor asleep, but filled with strange images and stranger voices. From time to time, it seemed to her that she rose very high and fell, light as a feather and drifting, very low.

Once she opened her eyes and a strange woman was standing above her, trying to make her drink something that was warm and strong. Another time, she thought she saw Merlin bending over her, looking grave. Another time it was a strange man in a dark coat. Each time she awakened, she drifted immediately back into sleep again, or an unconsciousness that was like sleep in a sea of night and stars and blackness.

Once or twice, she tried to struggle away from it, to rise to the surface. but she always failed.

And then, at last, she slept a true sleep, deep and sound.

And she slept for a long time.

10

"*I feel,*" *Lady* Wellford said weakly, but distinctly, "as if a stone wall had fallen on me."

"In a manner of speaking, it has," said a familiar voice.

She opened her eyes to see Lord Merlin's rugged features regarding her with a smile. He was in his shirtsleeves and there were dark rings beneath his eyes. A shaft of sunlight fell behind him, casting a soft illumination about his dark hair. It looked to her at that moment like an aura.

"I've died and gone to heaven," she said, closing her eyes again.

"No, but you are at Merlinford," he said cheerfully. "Drink this."

Strong arms supported her as she sat up, and she

sipped something cool and refreshing. It made her throat burn a little less, and she sighed gratefully, sinking back into the pillows. "That was wonderful," she whispered. "Why am I at Merlinford?"

And then she remembered. "Susan! Where is she? Did they reach Gretna?" Weakly, she struggled to sit up again, but strong hands pushed her gently back into the pillows.

"Susan is perfectly well and still Miss Dysart, not Mrs. Shelby. As it turns out, she only went as far as the Shelbys' house. Charlotte Shelby has her in her care at this very moment."

"Stupid girl," Audrey said succinctly.

"I am inclined to agree with you that Miss Dysart is a ninny. But our concern right now is you, Audrey."

"I've been sick, haven't I?" Audrey asked.

"As a matter of fact, yes," Merlin replied. "Very sick indeed. But you are looking much more the thing today."

"I am never ill," Audrey said stubbornly.

"You were very sick indeed. Influenza, you know. You had a high fever, and you were delirious."

Audrey digested this information without comment, for once silent.

She opened her eyes and studied Merlin thoughtfully. "I am so tired. And very thirsty."

He sat on the edge of the bed and helped her into a reclining position. From a carafe on a table beside the bed, he poured some liquid into a glass and held it to her lips. Audrey sipped.

When she finished, she leaned against his shoulder, unable to move. "I feel so dizzy," she murmured.

"You were very sick." He did not withdraw his support, but allowed her to rest against him. Frail as she felt, she was conscious of feeling quite secure in his presence. "I must look awful," she croaked.

"You don't look ravishing. You looked ravished."

"I was afraid of that."

"You need to rest now."

"Don't go. This is so comfortable," Audrey heard herself saying. And leaning against his big strong shoulder, she drifted off to sleep again, holding one of his big hands in her own. A little smile played about her lips. Asleep, she looked very angelic.

Merlin sighed, smiled, and made himself as comfortable as he could. He reached for a copy of *The Gentleman's Magazine,* which lay close to his free hand, turning the pages as best he could.

Mrs. Gowe, the Merlinford housekeeper, who was sitting quietly in the corner darning linen, smiled, but said nothing. Her busy needle flashed in and out of the sheet, glittering in the late afternoon sunlight.

"I think she's better, don't you?" he asked softly.

"Oh, much better, my lord," she replied.

When Audrey awakened again, long purple shadows of twilight were stretching across the room, and Merlin was dozing in his chair, a copy of the *Times* rising and falling on his chest.

She sat up in bed and found that she was in a strange nightgown, several sizes too large.

"Oh, you're awake," said a plump, pleasant-faced woman in a crisply starched mobcap. "How do you feel?"

Audrey blinked at her. "As if I've been through the wars."

The woman clucked her tongue. "And no wonder, for you were very ill. I'm Mrs. Gowe, the housekeeper. Do you think you could sip a little chicken broth?"

If his lordship's sudden and unannounced arrival at Merlinford in a pouring rain with a delirious lady in tow had surprised her, Mrs. Gowe had given no sign of it. Perhaps she had grown inured to the eccentricities of the clan through years of service to the old lord. A woman of extreme common sense, Mrs. Gowe had immediately set about to nurse Lady Wellford back to health.

Audrey wrinkled her nose. "Yes, please," she said meekly, however. "How long have I been ill?" she asked.

"Just two days." Mrs. Gowe pulled the bell, and when a maid appeared, "His lordship gave orders for a tray to be brought up to my lady."

"Poor Merlin," Audrey said. "He must be fagged to death."

"Oh, he's been by your bedside through most of it, as much as we would let him," Mrs. Gowe said, gazing fondly upon him. "The young lord was very concerned. Nothing would do but that he had to give you your barley water himself and be sure he was there if you awakened. Quite the nurse he is. Of course, there's not much staff at the house right now, it's been closed so long, so we all have to pitch in."

"Him?" Audrey breathed, incredulous. Were they talking about the same person?

"Oh, yes," the housekeeper said. "When he was in India, he went through a terrible epidemic, you know. He's one as knows just what to do, even the doctor said so."

Audrey still found that hard to believe, but it was only necessary to look at Mrs. Gowe to know that she never told a lie. Nonetheless, it gave Audrey something to think about as she sipped her chicken broth and watched him snooze, listening to his slight snoring rattle the pages of the newspaper.

"The young lord has barely snatched an hour's sleep since you came," Mrs. Gowe added. "He's taken care of you as if you was his own."

Merlin slept on, only reluctantly allowing himself to be roused when Dr. Crisp arrived.

The doctor, bustling in, informed her that he could have done no better himself. There was plenty of influenza around, and it was best to make the patient comfortable and allow it to run its course. Since Lady Wellford was young and in robust health, he was sanguine about her recovery.

"What you need, my lady, is rest and plenty of it," he advised after looking at her eyes, throat, and hands and taking her pulse. "And when you are stronger, good country milk and vegetables. You would not have been so sick had you not been worn to the bone."

Since he had known her when she was a girl at Bleakfriars, on the other side of the county, he addressed her familiarly, shaking his head and censuring town life as unhealthy and dangerous. "No doubt you've been gadding about far too much for your own good. Merlin tells me you've brought out Miss Susan! More gadding about, late hours and bad air!" He made notes in his little black volume. "Well, Merlin tells me you've gotten her a husband, so there's no reason for you to go jaunting back to London anytime soon! In fact, I am giving strict orders that you not be moved from this house until you are fully recovered. I've told Lord Merlin to have some of your things sent up from London. You're not going anywhere."

Audrey was feeling far too weak to argue with him. Besides, she was relieved that she would be spared neighborhood gossip.

No one could argue with Dr. Crisp!

The next day Audrey was allowed to get out of bed for a brief period of time. She sat in a wooden chair covered with a sheet and allowed Mrs. Gowe and one of the housemaids to fuss over her with a sponge, a cake of soap, and a basin of hot water.

"We need to wash your hair, but not quite yet," the housekeeper said, "for, in spite of the warm weather, you are still likely to take a chill, my lady! No tempting fate! We'll clean it today with corn-meal, the way we used to do when I was a girl. His lordship's sent a groom with the trap to town for your clothes, and I daresay they'll be here by tea, but in the meantime, no sense in risking a chill." The windows were closed firmly against a beautiful summer day and a fire was ignited in the grate in spite of the warm weather. Audrey was too exhausted to protest, and allowed them to bathe her, brush cornmeal through her hair, and install her in an armchair by the fire in one of Mrs. Gowe's clean nightgowns and Lord Merlin's embroidered dressing gown.

Only after they had finished was Merlin allowed admittance to the room, and Mrs. Gowe made a point of installing herself discreetly, if vigilantly, in a corner with her omnipresent mending.

Merlin, attired in buckskins, a smock, and a pair of short boots, thrust his head around the door. "Is it safe?" he asked, and upon her assent, entered the room.

"Forgive my dirt," he said, sinking into an opposite chair by the fire. His farmer's smock, open at the neck, exposed a thatch of brunet hair and an expanse of well-formed muscle. Audrey studied him appreciatively from beneath her lashes.

"We're opening ditches around the south pasture. It's shocking how neglected the pastures are here. My uncle cared very little for agriculture, it would seem. Or indeed, anything else." He gestured around the room at the faded wallpaper and threadbare curtains. "I haven't had a chance to do much about bringing the house into shape, as you can see. That needs a woman's touch. The land is something I can learn to manage, but I've never been much for household fripperies."

He crossed one leg over the other and thrust a hand into his pocket. He produced a tiny carving of a woman with six arms. "Here. Something I thought you might like to have." He tossed it carelessly toward her.

Audrey caught it, examining it with interest. Hewn from some soft stone, it gleamed faintly in her hand, warming to her touch.

"Kali, the cosmic dancer," he explained. "She's one of the principal goddesses of the Hindu pantheon."

"You told me about her. She has so many arms!"

"The better to sweep away the things of this world." He leaned back, regarding her pleasure in this small gift with a smile. "She's also Shiva the Destroyer, a most formidable lady."

"And not one I should like to cross," Audrey said seriously, placing the little carving carefully on the table. "Thank you. I shall treasure her."

They looked at each other for a moment, suddenly and oddly shy, then Merlin cleared his throat.

"Dr. Crisp put my head out for washing. Gave me merry hell for dragging you down here in the rain to see this place," he said with a careful sidelong glance at Mrs. Gowe in the corner. "Said I ought to know better, and I suppose he's right. Have you got everything you need? I sent one of the grooms to town to fetch back your woman and some clothes. I trust she'll know what to pack."

"Oh, yes, Wescott is a complete hand," Audrey said, nodding. She picked at the sleeve of his embroidered dressing gown. "I have you to thank, I understand, for looking after me, Merlin," she said slowly.

He shrugged. "I've been through worse, in India. We had a cholera epidemic that nearly carried me off. So I know something about nursing, as marvelous as that may seem to you. You look charming in that dressing gown. Perhaps I should make you a present of it?"

"And deprive you of it? Heavens, no!" It occurred to her that she had not looked in a mirror in days. "I must look like a quiz," she said, ducking her head.

"I just said that you looked charmingly." He frowned. "And you do. I don't have the compliments of a town beau, you know. In spite of all your good advice, I'm still no polished courtier."

"No," Audrey agreed with a little smile. "But then I must hardly be a lady of fashion right now, either. Instead, I must be a great hindrance to you, getting you into this. I'm truly sorry, Merlin. "

He shook his head. "It's hard to talk me into anything I don't want to do, you know."

Audrey sat up straight, possessed by a thought. "Have you heard anything about Appie? And how is Susan doing? Oh, Merlin, the ball—"

He held up a hand. "Dr. Crisp's orders. You are not to worry yourself about anything. We'll have all the news when your woman comes, I have no doubt. Miss Fishbank can never be too ill to communicate all the latest town topics, I'm sure. And speaking of worry, I have been strictly enjoined not to tease you overmuch, so I will take my leave."

With that, Audrey had to be content. Truth to tell, she was too frail to invest a great deal of worry into it just then. She did not even protest when Mrs. Gowe led her back to bed, saying she must conserve her strength. For once in her life, Audrey was too fragile to protest being fussed over.

Toward late afternoon, a carriage pulled up in the drive and Miss Fishbank, attired in a sensible bombazine traveling pelisse, stepped out to be greeted by Lord Merlin.

"Dear me! If Audrey had been with anyone other than you, I might have been quite distracted with worry," she said immediately. "When I received your note, I came at once. There was no sense in Wescott's coming, you see! I've had this affliction, and she has not! How does Audrey do?"

"She's recovering nicely," Merlin assured her. "I had no idea that she was ill until we were well on the road! I would never have allowed her to come on this journey if I had had the faintest hint that she was not well!"

"I must go to her at once!" Miss Fishbank pronounced as one who knew where her duties lay. "Does she know about our little scheme?"

Merlin looked sheepish. "No! She has been so sick—and I am a coward!" He grimaced, shaking his head. "I feel as if this imbroglio were all my fault! I could have killed her!"

"Nonsense! Audrey is as healthy as a horse! It would take more than a little influenza to put her low!" Miss Fishbank said briskly. "In fact, this may be a blessing in disguise."

"How?" Merlin asked doubtfully.

"We'll see," Miss Fishbank replied vaguely. "I should go up to her. Will you have someone bring up her trunk?"

Audrey looked unexpectedly fragile sitting up in the middle of the carved Jacobean bed. Without her rouge pot and her Lotion of the Ladies of Denmark, she looked surprisingly childlike.

"Appie!" she cried joyfully. "Oh, I am so glad to see you!"

Miss Fishbank drew off her gloves and undid the strings of her bonnet. "And I am very glad to see you, too! Dreadful stuff, this influenza! Half of London is down with it, and right in the middle of the Season, too! I thought it best that I came! Wescott, you know, has not had it yet, but I have!"

Audrey introduced her to Mrs. Gowe, who seemed almost visibly relieved to find a respectable female from Audrey's camp had come to bear her company. The housekeeper immediately went to procure refreshment and see that the adjoining bedroom was made up for the new company.

Once they were alone, Miss Fishbank sat down on the edge of the bed and felt Audrey's forehead.

"Oh, Appie, I'm not as sick as all of that," Audrey said impatiently, "no matter what Dr. Crisp says!" She giggled. "Merlin wants to wrap me in cotton wool, that's all!"

"Dr. Crisp! Is he still in practice? As good as any

of these London doctors, he is so very full of good advice," Miss Fishbank said. "That is a relief, to know you've been in good hands. But of course, when I discovered that you were with Nicholas, I did not worry. I knew that he could make everything come about."

"Yes, I suppose so! To his credit, he has been a most faithful nurse, they tell me. Who would have thought it of him?"

"Nicholas is a man of many talents," Miss Fishbank said cryptically. "Well, my dear, we shall do just as Dr. Crisp tells us, and you'll be as right as a trivet!"

"No doubt, but what about Susan? I have been lying here thinking it all over, and I am convinced that she and Giles will suit very well. That girl will do very well as a soldier's wife, don't you think?"

"Then you are not upset?"

"Why should I be? Well, yes I am, for two reasons. One is that they should have said something sooner and spared us all this fiasco, and the other is that they should not have eloped! That was most improper!"

Miss Fishbank's lips twitched. "Well, she wanted to elope, as I understand it, but the major would have none of it! Once he found out which way the wind was blowing, he took her right off to his mother's house. I understand that he gave his sisters a great set-down also, for causing you so much grief at Vauxhall, which was most improper of them. I don't need to tell you that Mrs. Shelby is most appalled, but also most pleased at her prospective daughter-in-law."

"Well, that removes both of them from my hands. Lord, Appie, but Giles Shelby is the most tiresome, pompous bobbing block I ever met in my life! Why didn't you *warn* me?"

"Would you have listened if I did?" Miss Fishbank asked mildly.

"No," Audrey confessed readily. "I would have shrugged it off! Like the fool I am! I never thought I would be so pleased to be cast off! That's two problems solved at once! We may announce their engagement at the ball, which, Dr. Crisp or no Dr. Crisp, I *will* be in town to attend."

"All the invitations have been sent out and the acceptances are pouring in. It will be a dreadful squeeze, I fear."

"Perfect! A dreadful squeeze is precisely what we wish for! Has Monsieur Levec been in touch with you?"

"He assures me that all is well, and everything is going according to plan. What an extraordinary little man!"

Audrey sank back against the pillows. "I feel like a perfect fool," she admitted. "I should have seen what was going on under my very nose!"

"This is not the time to worry about these things," Miss Fishbank said reassuringly. "You concentrate on getting well now."

"Merlin thinks I am a fool," Audrey fretted. "I have misjudged him very badly, I think. No one who is totally selfish and odious and rude would ever show as much consideration as he has! When I needed him, he was right here!"

"Yes, Nicholas is all that is admirable," Miss Fishbank soothed her. "He's the sort of man one can count on!"

Was it possible that Audrey was beginning to see the light?

Miss Fishbank had cause to wonder over the next several days. As soon as Dr. Crisp agreed, she was allowed to come downstairs and lie on a chaise longue on the terrace. Wrapped in blankets and shawls in spite of the sunny weather, holding her parasol against the rays of the sun, she watched Lord Merlin escort Miss Fishbank through the formal boxwoods, pointing out all the features of the Capability Brown gardens.

It was, she decided, perfectly lovely not to have anything to do or any place to go. With some surprise, she realized that she had not missed the endless rounds of shopping, socializing, and pleasure-seeking that defined her London life. Sitting here in the sun, it all seemed very far away and very empty. She *especially* did not miss the constrictions of chaperoning a debutante through the Byzantine labyrinths of rigid propriety!

She stretched and sighed. She supposed she should regret losing Giles, but she did not. As ornamental as he was, and he was undeniably a most handsome man, but—! Well, truth to tell, his understanding was *not* profound, and that, if nothing else, made him perfect for Susan, who was never going to set the world on fire with her brilliance, either. Doubtless, they would deal extremely well together, and produce a brood of good-looking, rather dull children. Certainly, Charlotte Shelby would be happy to have her as a daughter-in-law. Susan had found a loving family at last. By now, she was probably more Shelby than Dysart, and it must seem to them all as if she had been in the family forever. If only Audrey had not been so determined to manage everyone's lives, she might have seen more clearly what was happening right beneath her nose!

Could it be that Audrey was not as clever as she thought herself to be? This was a novel, if uncomfortable, thought for the fashionable Lady Wellford. She was never a great one for introspective thought. One never knew where it might lead, or what painful changes one might have to make. And there was nothing Audrey disliked more than being uncomfortable or feeling as if she were not the mistress of her own destiny.

As if he sensed that she was thinking about him, Lord Merlin looked up and smiled at her. He was not handsome, she thought, nor was he fashionable. His coat and plain buckskins were neat rather than stylish, and there was no high sheen to his boots. His address, as she had good reason to know, was not polished, his manners could be deplorable, and when his temper was aroused—well, he was utterly impossible then.

But in the past few days, he had shown another side of himself, a more gentle, more comfortable aspect of himself that she could not help but like. There was more to him than mere *style;* he had strength and substance. Merlin had shown himself to be capable and dependable. And he could make her laugh.

He said something to Miss Fishbank and the two of them began to walk back up the gravel path toward the terrace. Appie liked him, she noted. Appie, who rarely appreciated any of Audrey's beaux, seemed to have taken to him wholeheartedly. Now *that* was interesting.

"You must stroll in the gardens when you are able to take some exercise," Miss Fishbank said. "Lord Merlin has some lovely old roses."

"And Miss Fishbank has been kind enough to

share her expertise with me," Merlin said. "I have charged her with conveying her suggestions to my gardener."

Miss Fishbank glanced at the watch on her breast. "Dear me, is it lunch time already? I should go and tell Mrs. Gowe that we will be eating on the terrace today. It's such a lovely day, too." She bustled off, looking quite pleased with herself.

"It is time for you to take a little exercise," Merlin said. "A turn about the Italian water garden is just what the doctor would like."

Before Audrey could protest, he had handed her to her feet, divested her of her numerous rugs and shawls and was leading her down the steps and into the garden.

"My uncle made the Grand Tour, the way they used to do, and fell in love with Italian gardens. Nothing would do but he had to tear up the entire south lawn and convert it into a series of jets, fountains, and displays." Merlin explained. "Hence, as you can see, there is a great deal of statuary. You will note that there is much of it that is deplorable—" he broke off, then continued in a more serious tone. "Audrey, there is something I need to discuss with you. You see, I—"

There was a silver chiming, and Merlin paused. "It sounds as if lunch is being served," he finished lamely.

"Then I suppose we'd best go back to the house," Audrey said. "What is it you want to talk to me about?"

"Oh, nothing that can't wait," Merlin said with some relief. *Nick, you are a coward!* he thought to himself. *You've faced pirates, floods, bandits, epidemics, and*

*murders in your career, but you can't tell a woman
the simple truth!*

"I thought perhaps you might—like to see the
picture gallery," he finished lamely. "After lunch I
could take you on a tour. The pictures at Merlinford
are said to be some of the best in any of the country
houses."

"It is a lovely house. We never came here when I
was growing up. By then, my brother had managed
to quarrel dreadfully with almost everyone in the
neighborhood. So this is my first chance to see the
house. I just never dreamed that I would be an invalid
here."

"And how do you feel today?"

"As if I could take a gallop across country and
then eat the horse! Unfortunately, my abigail did not
pack a habit for me."

"I could take you for a drive, however. I am sure
that Dr. Crisp would agree that a gentle jaunt down
country lanes would be most healthful!" He grinned.

"Besides, I would give almost anything to handle
those fine bays of yours!" Audrey said.

"Almost anything?" Merlin asked lightly.

"Why, sir, I do believe you are flirting with me!"
Audrey laughed. She squeezed his arm.

"Why, you know that I am too much of a
booberkin to know how to flirt," Merlin replied. "If
I were one of your polished town beaux, I would ask
you for a bribe to drive my team!"

"What sort of a bribe did you have in mind?"
Audrey asked lightly.

Merlin cleared his throat. "A kiss—" he started to
say, but before the words were out of his mouth, Miss
Fishbank appeared from behind the Italian larches.

"There you two are! Come now, lunch will be cold if you dawdle!" she commanded. "And Mrs. Gowe will be sadly out of sorts, for she has made a crab pie!"

Merlin sighed and allowed Audrey to lead him back to the terrace.

He had to admit, however, that it was a very good crab pie.

11

"*You know, Merlin, I have* been thinking," Audrey said.

They were driving down a country lane near Hand Cross in his curricle. Audrey held the reins and guided the bays at a spanking pace.

"And what have you been thinking?" Merlin asked lazily. It was another gloriously sunny day, and the hedgerows were full of blooms. Across the rolling hills, fields of green wheat waved in the breeze, and cattle grazed peacefully in the square fields.

"About the Season. People go to their town houses in May and June and July in London, and meanwhile, the country is at its loveliest! And then, they come back to the country in August and stay there all winter, when the country is at its most dead. Does that make any sense to you?"

"None whatsoever," he replied easily.

Although Audrey was completely restored to health within a few days of her first falling ill, she had made no move to return to London. Far from the madding crowd, they might have been living on a desert island. Life had fallen into a pleasant routine. The day started with breakfast and the newspapers, and then Merlin saw to his land or consulted with his bailiff and tenants. After lunch, they took his curricle out, while Miss Fishbank snoozed in the drawing room with a novel, and after dinner, they walked in the gardens. When it got dark, they played cutthroat card games for fabulous, if utterly imaginary, stakes. It was a gentle, peaceful existence, and Audrey was never bored.

"Do you know that we have not quarreled once since I came here?" she asked Merlin.

"I am doing my best to be as nonodious as possible," he replied gravely. In fact, he was more relaxed and at ease than she had ever seen him.

"And I am doing my best to not be managing!"

For her part, Audrey found doing without Wescott or an extensive wardrobe in the country no great hardship. She brushed her own hair and tied it back in a simple style and sometimes wore the same morning dress through the whole day, not even changing for dinner. Her fashionable friends such as Madam Hart would have been surprised to see how simply she went about her day and how much pleasure she had from the simplest things. Country bred, Audrey found it easy to return to the bucolic manners of her childhood, but with the difference that at Merlinford, she was finding a peace she had not previously known.

"I would think that Merlinford would be slow for

your tastes," Merlin observed. "With all the state rooms in holland covers and only a handful of staff, no balls, nor parties, no gay company, it must seem decidedly flat."

"Well, I have been thinking," Audrey said. "It seems almost everyone on your staff yearns for the good old days when the old lord entertained lavishly. Mrs. Gowe says they used to have upwards of thirty or forty here during the hunting season."

"Did they! That was before my time!" Merlin stretched out his long legs. "When I was a boy, my aunt had already died. This place"—he gestured over the hill toward the old Jacobean pile—"was already as gloomy as an abandoned temple in a distant jungle."

"Well, you know, I have been thinking, that if you took your seat in the House, you'd have to start entertaining again."

"Very true, if I meant to make a great push of it."

"There's no reason why you shouldn't be a public man," Audrey said thoughtfully.

"I would of course need a suitable wife for that," Merlin said.

"I am sure there are many females who would be delighted to accept your suit."

"What makes you think so?"

"Why, Merlin! Are you fishing for compliments?"

"No, I am casting my hook out in hopes of snaring a wife."

"Well, I certainly wish you luck in that endeavor."

"Audrey, for a dreadfully managing female, you can be damned obtuse!" he exclaimed gruffly.

"Perhaps I should have mentioned our not quarreling," she said. "It's such a lovely day, Merlin, let's not come to blows right now!"

Feeling very frustrated indeed, Merlin thrust his hands into his pockets and frowned. Where, he wondered, was his courage?

Unfortunately, he did not have long to discover it.

When they arrived back at Merlinford, there was a strange chaise in the driveway.

"It looks as if we have visitors," Audrey said.

Merlin frowned. "I wonder who that could be."

They did not have to wait in suspense for very long. As soon as they were inside the door, Mrs. Gowe, bearing a tray with a bottle of Madeira and a plate of macaroons, bustled up to them, beaming.

"Oh, sir, my lady, it's Miss Dysart from Bleakfrairs!" she said.

Merlin and Audrey exchanged a glance. "I hope you only have the one niece," he said to Audrey beneath his breath. "No more in the schoolroom that I missed?"

"So do I!" Audrey retorted. "I don't think I could go through this twice!"

But it was Susan, looking very fetching in a traveling pelisse and a new high-crowned bonnet. She was accompanied by the major. They had been talking to Miss Fishbank, but when Audrey came into the room, she jumped up and cast herself over her aunt.

"Oh, I hope you will forgive me," she exclaimed. "I am the most ungrateful wretch alive!"

The major also rose to his feet, turning a deep crimson. "I told her, I said, 'Susan, our duty is clear. Before we go another step, we must come and apologize to your aunt for all that she's been through. And of course, we must thank Lord Merlin, for if it were not for him, we never would have gotten buckled, nor been so happy.'"

"Gotten buckled?" Audrey asked, gently disentangling Susan from about her neck. "Do you mean that you're married?"

By way of answer, Susan held up her left hand to display a thin gold band. "Please wish us happy! We are on our way to Bleakfriars so that Giles may meet Mama and Papa, and then we are taking the next packet to India. Giles's regiment has been ordered out, and thanks to Lord Merlin, he is to be promoted to colonel!"

"What?" Audrey turned to Merlin, all at sea.

Merlin was turning a very dark red, and, she saw, was to be of no help at all. The man was obviously in shock. "When did you get married?" she asked. "Though of course, I wish you well—no need to ask me forgiveness, I think you two shall do very well together, but—"

"Didn't Merlin tell you?" Susan asked. Bathed in the glow of newlywed bliss, she smiled blissfully at Giles, who blew her a kiss.

"We were married by special license as soon as Lord Merlin bought Giles's commission. We used the special license Sir Peyton and Madam Hart had procured, because Lord Merlin was afraid that if we did not get married right away, Papa would put a stop to it! But now that we are married, Mama and Papa have forgiven me, and I am taking Giles to meet them—"

Audrey must have been looking very strange indeed, for Susan stopped in midsentence and took a step or two away from her. "Are you quite well, Aunt Audrey? You look so strange."

"Audrey, please don't be angry with us," Giles said, taking a step forward and placing a protective arm about his bride's shoulders. "It was love at first sight! Well, second sight, at any rate. But—"

"Oh, it's not you that I'm angry with," Audrey said, managing to keep her voice under control. "You will forgive me if I seem to be ignorant of everything Lord Merlin has accomplished!"

"Isn't he the most complete hand?" Susan asked, gazing fondly up at Major Shelby.

He blew her kisses. "We owe our present happiness to his good offices," he said. "So, we had to come by and thank you, sir. And to wish you and Audrey all the best!"

"The best of what?" Audrey asked blankly.

"Audrey, I can explain," Merlin said a little desperately. "I have meant to explain all along—"

"No need, I think it is all clear to me now," Audrey replied coldly. "You seem to have managed this all just wonderfully without me." She looked over at Miss Fishbank, who had the grace to look distinctly uncomfortable. "So, your elopement was a Banbury tale, made up to lure me out of town while you went behind my back and—*you planned all of this!*"

"Audrey, it's not what you think it is! I've been trying to tell you—" Merlin frowned. He passed a hand around his collar, as if it were too tight. "Well, damn, I had to!"

"Of course you did! It was all a hum, but to what purpose? What else have you been doing that I don't know about? And why? Is this your idea of a joke, or a way of proving yourself right, that I could never manage to fire my niece off into the ton because I'm too *fast?*" she asked.

"Audrey, please listen to me! I wanted to tell you, but first you became sick, which believe me I had not counted on, and then things were going so well between us that I—"

"It was all a hum to get me up here to Merlinford!" Audrey cried, full of indignation.

"It was all a hum to get you up to Merlinford so that I could ask you to marry me!" Merlin roared. "I thought it would only be for the day! I thought that if I could get you away from all the distractions in London, I might be able to convince you that you love me as much as I love you!"

"Well, I do love you! But I wouldn't marry you if you were the last man in England!"

With that, Audrey slammed out of the room.

Susan stared at the door. "Did I say something wrong?" she asked.

12

"*She was* almost *ready to forgive* Merlin, I think, when Susan and the major appeared—so unfortunate . . ." Miss Fishbank informed Madam Hart. "Well, you may imagine what her reaction was then!"

The two women were standing in the morning room. As they were talking, one of the footmen passed the door, bearing an enormous arrangement of flowers. "This place looks like someone died," Emma said frankly. "All you need is some crepe on the door knocker and some straw in the street. "

Miss Fishbank looked around herself, nodding assent. Every flat surface, every table, every stand was filled with huge bouquets. "We're beginning to run out of vases and places to put them," she said. "And he just keeps sending more. And he calls, but she refuses to see him! I cannot comprehend it! She says that she loves him, and she knows, or she ought to by now, that he loves her, but she refuses to see him! It is excessively—*stupid!* Of all Audrey's fits and starts, this has to be the strangest! If only that silly chit had simply stayed at Bleakfriars, none of this would have happened! And now, we have this ball, and nosegays are arriving for that, and *I am quite distracted!*"

"Oh, that silly ball! Is she going?"

"I don't know," Miss Fishbank replied frankly. "She's not speaking to me." She sniffed. "I have packed my things to go to my sister's house in Bath until this blows over! She hasn't come out of her room since Sally Jersey was here." She gestured toward the trunk in the hallway. "I am only waiting for the post chaise!"

"That one must have enjoyed stirring the pot!" Madam Hart muttered.

"Doubtless. I've never seen Audrey in such a taking! Oh, she said some things that were terrible and smashed an Imari vase!"

Madam Hart nodded, readjusting a shawl that had fallen from one shoulder. "Yes, it sounds like the mad scene I played in *Castle Dread!* I was marvelous, if I do say so myself." She squared her shoulders. "Well, let me go upstairs and see what I can do. If anyone can persuade some sense into her, I can."

"I've done *my* best," Miss Fishbank said darkly.

Majestically, Emma mounted the stairs and proceeded down the hall where she encountered Wescott and Otterbine standing outside Audrey's bedroom door. Otterbine held a tray, Wescott had a dress thrown over one arm. Both of them looked extremely worried.

"My lady, you must eat something," Otterbine was

saying. "You didn't touch your breakfast or your dinner last night!"

"My lady, in case you have forgotten, you are the hostess of this here ball this evening, and if you don't show up, you know what will happen!"

When they saw Madam Hart, both of them looked much relieved and began talking to her all at once. "She won't come out!" "A full-dress ball tonight, all of London coming, and she won't come out!"

"She hasn't touched a bite since lunch yesterday! She won't answer the door," Otterbine agonized. "What shall we do?"

The diva stepped up and rapped smartly on the panels. "Audrey! Let me in! It's Emma! I want a word with you, and if I don't get it, I'm going to have Otterbine and the footmen take the door off the hinges!"

Silence.

"I have never been more sincere, Audrey! If you don't think I won't do it, try me!"

This achieved the desired effect. The door opened a crack and Emma, ever one to seize the advantage, thrust her way in, slamming it firmly behind her.

"You look dreadful," she said flatly.

"What did you have to do with all of this?" Audrey demanded. "Since everyone else has been involved in a conspiracy to match me up with Merlin, I have no doubt that you and Peyton did, too." She did not look her best, it was true. There were dark circles under her eyes and she was as pale as the ivory muslin gown she wore.

"If you don't have enough common sense to act in your own behalf, then you'd best allow your friends to work for you. Good God, what are you doing?"

Emma looked about the room, where drawers were opened and things strewn everywhere.

"I'm going to Paris." She scooped up a handful of papers. "Do you think I can stay here when everyone in London knows what a fool I've been?"

"What? A fool? You?" Emma asked incredulously.

"Trying to become respectable! Hellfire and brimstone!" Audrey sank into a chair, crushing a peau de soie dinner dress beneath her. "And all the while, Merlin was behind the scenes, masterminding the whole thing! Odious! Everyone in town must be laughing at me! I cannot abide being humbugged!"

"But we all meant well. It's as clear as water that you and Merlin are meant for each other, Audrey."

Lady Wellford pushed a hand through her tangled hair. "That's the worst part of it! He arranged everything so that I would go out of town with him on a hum! He made it seem as if Giles and Susan were eloping to Scotland so I would pursue them! And he was right there! Right there when I came out the door! I dropped into his hands like a ripe plum! He tried to trick me! He thought that if he could get me alone, I would fall in love with him! And the thing is, I did!"

"Ah, now we're getting somewhere!" Emma said. She peered into Audrey's furious expression. "No one thought you would come down with the influenza, you know. The idea was to separate you from Susan so that Merlin could declare himself. It was meant for an afternoon only."

Audrey looked up at Emma from beneath her hair. "You knew all about this, too! All of my *soi-disant* friends knew about it! You and Emma and Sally! How could you? *How could any of you?*"

"Well, someone had to do it! Audrey, you've been

managing everyone else's lives forever, but when it comes to your own, you don't know what you're doing! Here is the man for you, and you can't even see it."

"Well, I thought he was the man for me until I found out he'd been scheming behind my back! Emma, you of all people ought to comprehend how much I abhor any attempt to curb my independence! He assumed that I was in a situation I couldn't handle so he assumed he had to help me out of it! But he did it behind my back—and with the full cooperation of my friends!"

"If it were a play, it would be by Sheridan," the actress replied, in no way discomfited. A hardened campaigner in the treacherous world of theatrical politics, she was made of stronger stuff than Miss Fishbank. "Besides, if it were left to you, Susan would be lounging about the house in tears, Giles would be sulking, and you would have been miserably attempting to be respectable until you lost your temper and did something you would regret. Which is what is happening right now." She sank into the chair by the escritoire and opened a silver dish hopefully. It did indeed contain chocolate comfits. She popped one into her mouth.

"If you don't stop eating those things, you are going to be too fat to get into any of your costumes," Audrey said nastily.

"I know what you are afraid of," Emma observed, helping herself to another one. From the floor, she picked up a waterloo bonnet, high-crowned and trimmed with a great deal of ribbon. She removed her own chip straw leghorn and placed the bonnet on her head, looking this way and that in the pier glass opposite. "You are afraid of being in love."

"I'm not afraid of anything," Audrey said, put she propped her hand into her chin and looked dubious.

"You remind me of myself when I played Clarissa in *The Beau's Revenge*. Clarissa, you see, is pursued by Danton, but she really loves Mr. Bold, so—"

"This is my life, not a play!" Audrey exclaimed impatiently. "And I'm not afraid of being in love!"

"Then why are you running away from the one man who can make you happy? Audrey, I know you and I know you're not as hard and jaded as you would have the world believe you are!"

"If I was not before, I am now," Audrey said. "The one time I trust someone, the one time I let myself fall in love with a man—he tricks me!"

"Well, you could at least talk to him. Have you seen all those flowers down there?"

Audrey shook her head. "I don't want to talk to him! If I talk to him, he'll convince me I'm in love with him! He might want me to *marry* him, and then what would I do?"

"Well, if that's what you have to do to keep him, then I should very strongly suggest you do it! Men like Merlin don't grow on trees, you know," Emma said wisely. "Look how long it took me to find a man like Peyton." Emma rose, replacing her own hat on her head. "Audrey, let me tell you this, my dear." She turned this way and that looking at herself in the glass. "You can rustle on, making the world think you care for nothing but the latest styles and the next good-looking lover, but in the end, you're going to be a very lonely lady indeed. You've managed your family out of your life because you can't forgive, you've managed Susan and Giles out of your life because you can't forgive, and you're about to lose

Appie Fishbank, who has stood by you through thick and thin, because you can't bear to bend. And now, you're about to toss away the one man who can make you happy, because you can't bend. You and your pride are going to be very lonely, Audrey. Believe me, I know. Love isn't about controlling people, Audrey, it's about sharing. It's about accepting people for what they are, not what you want them to be." She tossed her shawl over her shoulder and walked to the door. "I hope you and your pride and your independence will be happy together. Because if you keep on going the way you have been, that's the company you're going to have for the rest of your life."

And with that speech, she closed the door behind her, leaving Audrey to stew.

"What did she say, miss?" Wescott asked.

"Is she hungry now?" Otterbine asked. "This has upset the entire household."

"I," Madam Hart said in ringing tones, "have done my duty. The next step is act two."

Otterbine sighed. "This is not at all what one is used to in a lady's household."

Wescott, however, stiffened her shoulders. "Just say the word, miss!"

Madam Hart smiled. "I knew we could count on you."

At eight o'clock, Otterbine tapped genteely at Audrey's door.

"My lady, I am sorry to disturb you," he said, without waiting for a response, "but there is a French person belowstairs who says he must have a word with you. He is quite insistent, my lady."

From within, there was only silence. Otterbine waited a moment, then cleared his throat. "He says it's a matter of life or death. His name is Monsieur Levec."

Audrey's door opened a crack. "What does he want?" she asked.

"He would only say that it is of the greatest urgency that he speak with you. I placed him in the Green Salon, my lady."

Audrey sighed, thought. Curiosity won out. "I suppose I had better come down. It might be something serious."

Monsieur Levec, resplendent in corbeau-colored formal evening attire, rose as Audrey entered the room. He looked extremely upset. He bowed low. "Ah, milady! Thank *le bon Dieu* that I have found you at home! You must come at once! All is in readiness *pour le bal* and then—" He spread his fingers eloquently. "Milord becomes ill! *Monsieur le docteur* is sent for. The situation is not good, he says. Milord is very, very ill. He has the fever, the—*comment on disais?*— eenfluenza. *C'est affreux!* He is very ill, milady, *avec la fièvere mauvaise.* He calls for you and we cannot help him! You must come at once!" Monsieur Levec mopped his brow with a scented handkerchief. "I remember when M. le Duc was like this. He did not survive. *C'est terrible.* You must come at once!"

"Oh, no you don't, Monsieur Levec!" Audrey said. "I will *not* be hoaxed again! You go back"—she took a step forward and poked her finger at Levec's elegant cravat—"you go back and tell him to hand some one else his Banbury stories! I have had quite enough!"

"*Mais,* milady—" Levec started to say.

He was too late. Picking up her skirts, Audrey flounced up the stairs. "If anyone else calls, Otterbine," she said coldly as she passed him on the stairs, "be good enough to tell them that *I am not at home!*"

Back in her room, as soon as she had closed the door behind her, Audrey sat down on the end of the chaise and burst into tears. The experience of tears was so novel that she did not know quite what to do, save give way to the misery that was overwhelming her. In all her life, Audrey had never felt so alone or uncertain. She picked up the little Shiva carving and turned it over in her hand.

She knew she was being foolish, that her pride was dooming her, but she also felt as if there were no way to stop what had been set in motion.

Her thoughts were cut by the sound of a muffled, masculine curse and the sound of breaking glass. A perfume vial shattered on the floor and the essence of roses permeated the room.

"Damn!"

As she watched, stunned, the window slowly opened, and a pair of hands gripped the sill. One leg looped over the sill. Slowly, a face appeared in the opening, looking a little foolish. "I'm not as young as I used to be. Can you give me a hand here?" Merlin asked, a little out of breath.

Audrey was suddenly laughing and crying at once. "You are—mad!" she exclaimed as she rose and threw open the sash, helping him to clamber awkwardly over the sill and into the boudoir.

"It looked so easy when Major Shelby did it," Merlin said, dusting himself off. "Climbing up vines is definitely not one of my talents!"

"Why aren't you home on your deathbed?" Audrey

started to ask, but Merlin had swept her into his arms and silenced her by the simple expedient of placing his lips over hers and holding her very tightly.

Audrey responded by wrapping her arms around his strong shoulders and returning his kiss with equal enthusiasm. Her toes curled inside her slippers as he lifted her off her feet and crushed her against his chest.

It was quite some time before either of them wanted or needed to speak.

"I was wrong," Merlin breathed.

"No, I was wrong!" Audrey asserted.

"Audrey Dysart, I love you! I have no airs or gallant manners with which to impress you, but I love you and I want to spend the rest of my life proving that to you," he said gruffly, smoothing her hair with his finger, still crushing her against his chest so tightly she could feel his heart beating against hers. "Is this the only way I can get you to listen to me? My little fool!"

"My *big* fool!" she sighed happily, and turned her face up to his for another kiss.

This one was even better than the first.

It lasted for quite a long time.

It melted through Audrey in a liquid tide of rippling fire.

"Dearest, managing love, will you marry me?" Merlin asked.

"Does it have to be marriage?" Audrey asked doubtfully.

"I want you to make a respectable man out of me. Damn it, Audrey, I can't keep climbing up vines and arranging plots all over the place! I'm too old for this!"

He kissed her again.

"I think I could become accustomed to this," Audrey said.

"It's you I want, my dearest. What else do I have to do to prove it?"

"I don't want to give up my independence. I don't want to be a possession."

"This is an equal match in every way! If it's your money you're worried about, have your man of business put it into a trust for our children, because we are going to have one or two of our own, I hope, and if they're anything like your shatterbrained niece, they will be very glad of your fortune."

He tilted her chin up to his gaze with his thumb.

"Oh, no! Our children will be perfect! Kiss me again," she commanded, closing her eyes.

"Always happy to oblige a lady," Merlin murmured.

Much, much later, she rested her head against his chest. "So this is what love is like. I was beginning to wonder."

"It is just the beginning, my love!" Merlin reassured her tenderly. "We can have a whole life together."

"Then I suppose I must marry you."

"It's the only way." Merlin grinned.

Audrey sighed. "Very well!" She looked up at him. "But you must promise me, no more Banbury tales!"

"No more, I swear!" He placed her hand on his heart. "No more nieces?"

"No more. Well, it does seem as if I have nephews named Frank and Barney, but I am sure that they will not need Seasons."

"I devoutly hope not! Preferences, commissions, positions, these things I am prepared to deal with, but no more debutantes!"

"I promise! I am so dreadfully tired of being

respectable. Merlin, are you sure that we have to get married?"

"Absolutely! I want to be certain that you will not be casting about for any more big, blond, stupid military men!"

"I am hideously expensive, you know! If you saw my dress bill every month you would be terribly upset!"

"I think I can stand the blunt. Double it, if that's what you want. But wait until we go to Paris! I will have no dowdy quiz of a wife who's not in the latest Parisian mode!"

"Paris?"

"Of course, Paris. Were else would you want to be married? We shall leave directly after the ball, at which I believe we really ought to put in some sort of an appearance lest Mrs. Shelby consider herself deserted!"

Audrey pouted. "Must we go?"

"Absolutely. I want to use the event to announce our engagement. And then, after we return from Paris and all the scandal has died down, we shall be quite dull and respectable."

"Besides, Monsieur Levec will be terribly put out after all his hard work! Oh, Merlin, how could you make him come over here tonight and tell that terrible lie?"

"I assure you, he enjoyed it thoroughly. Besides, I needed to distract you while I crawled up the vine and into your window. And if that piece of work don't convince you I love you, nothing will!"

"But what about Appie? She can't—"

"Miss Fishbank has gone to Bath to visit her sister. For a much-needed holiday from your antics, my treasure!"

"Oh, I suppose you are right. What a perfectly

puffed-up, prideful, odious person I am! What a perfect match for you!"

"I would have no other," Merlin declared solemnly.

They kissed yet again.

"Merlin," Audrey said thoughtfully, after a while, "I have been thinking. When you take your seat in the house and become an important public man, there are a number of persons you and I really ought to—"

"Yes, my managing beauty!" he laughed. "I can see now that whatever life with you will be like, it will never be dull!"

Rebecca Baldwin lives and works on the Eastern Shore of Maryland, where, under her pen name, she writes a column for the Baltimore *Sun*.

AVAILABLE NOW

FLAME LILY by Candace Camp

Continuing the saga of the Tyrells begun in *Rain Lily,* another heart-tugging, passionate tale of love from bestselling author Candace Camp. Returning home after years at war, Confederate officer Hunter Tyrell dreamed only of marrying his sweetheart, Linette Sanders, and settling down. But when he discovered that Linette had wed another, he vowed never to love again—until he found out her heartbreaking secret.

ALL THAT GLITTERS by Ruth Ryan Langan

From a humble singing job in a Los Angeles bar, Alexandra Corday is discovered and propelled into stardom. Along the way her path crosses that of rising young photographer Adam Montrose. Just when it seems that Alex will finally have it all—a man she loves, a home for herself and her brother, and the family she has always yearned for—buried secrets threaten to destroy her.

THE WIND CASTS NO SHADOW by Roslynn Griffith

With an incredibly deft hand, Roslynn Griffith has combined Indian mythology and historical flavor in this compelling tale of love, betrayal, and murder deep in the heart of New Mexico territory.

UNQUIET HEARTS by Kathy Lynn Emerson

Tudor England comes back to life in this richly detailed historical romance. With the death of her mother, Thomasine Strangeways had no choice but to return to Catsholme Manor, the home where her mother was once employed as governess. There she was reunited with Nick Carrier, her childhood hero who had become the manor's steward. Meeting now as adults, they found the attraction between them instant and undeniable, but they were both guarding dangerous secrets.

STOLEN TREASURE by Catriona Flynt

A madcap romantic adventure set in 19th-century Arizona gold country. Neel Blade was rich, handsome, lucky, and thoroughly bored, until he met Cate Stewart, a feisty chemist who was trying to hold her world together while her father was in prison. He instantly fell in love with her, but if only he could remember who he was . . .

WILD CARD by Nancy Hutchinson

It is a dream come true for writer Sarah MacDonald when movie idol Ian Wild miraculously appears on her doorstep. This just doesn't happen to a typical widow who lives a quiet, unexciting life in a small college town. But when Ian convinces Sarah to go with him to his remote Montana ranch, she comes face to face with not only a life and a love more exciting than anything in the pages of her novels, but a shocking murder.

COMING NEXT MONTH

STARLIGHT by Patricia Hagan
Another spellbinding historical romance from bestselling author Patricia Hagan. Desperate to escape her miserable life in Paris, Samara Labonte agreed to switch places with a friend and marry an American soldier. During the train journey to her intended, however, Sam was abducted by Cheyenne Indians. Though at first she was terrified, her heart was soon captured by one particular blue-eyed warrior.

THE NIGHT ORCHID by Patricia Simpson
A stunning new time travel story from an author who *Romantic Times* says is "fast becoming one of the premier writers of supernatural romance." When Marissa Quinn goes to Seattle to find her missing sister who was working for a scientist, what she finds instead is a race across centuries with a powerfully handsome Celtic warrior from 285 B.C. He is the key to her missing sister and the man who steals her heart.

ALL THINGS BEAUTIFUL by Cathy Maxwell
Set in the ballrooms and country estates of Regency England, a stirring love story of a dark, mysterious tradesman and his exquisite aristocratic wife looking to find all things beautiful. "*All Things Beautiful* is a wonderful 'Beauty and the Beast' story with a twist. Cathy Maxwell is a bright new talent."—*Romantic Times*

THE COMING HOME PLACE by Mary Spencer
Knowing that her new husband, James, loved another, Elizabeth left him and made a new life for herself. Soon she emerged from her plain cocoon to become an astonishingly lovely woman. Only when James' best friend ardently pursued her did James realize the mistake he had made by letting Elizabeth go.

DEADLY DESIRES by Christina Dair
When photographer Jessica Martinson begins to uncover the hidden history of the exclusive Santa Lucia Inn, she is targeted as the next victim of a murderer who will stop at nothing to prevent the truth from coming out. Now she must find out who is behind the murders, as all the evidence is pointing to the one man she has finally given her heart to.

MIRAGE by Donna Valentino
To escape her domineering father, Eleanor McKittrick ran away to the Kansas frontier where she and her friend Lauretta had purchased land to homestead. Her father, a prison warden, sent Tremayne Hawthorne, an Englishman imprisoned for a murder he didn't commit, after her in exchange for his freedom. Yet Hawthorne soon realized that this was a woman he couldn't bear to give up.

Harper Monogram **The Mark of Distinctive Women's Fiction**